PARADISE

Jill S. Alexander

D0005395

FEIWEL AND FRIENDS · NEW YORK

A FEIWEL AND FRIENDS BOOK
An Imprint of Macmillan

PARADISE. Copyright © 2011 by Jill S. Alexander. All rights reserved. Printed in May 2011 in the
United States of America by R. R. Donnelley & Sons Company, Harrisonburg, Virginia.
For information, address Feiwel and Friends, 175 Fifth Avenue, New York, N.Y. 10010.

Library of Congress Cataloging-in-Publication Data

Alexander, Jill (Jill Shurbet)
Paradise / Jill S. Alexander. — 1st ed.
p. cm.
Summary: Teenaged Paisley Tillery dreams a career as a professional drummer will take
her out of her small Texas town, but when her country rock band gets a handsome new
lead singer from Paradise, Texas, those dreams may change.
ISBN: 978-0-312-60541-4
[1. Bands (Music)—Fiction.   2. Drummers (Musicians)—Fiction.
3. Country rock music—Fiction.   4. Ambition—Fiction.   5. Love—Fiction.
6. Family life—Texas—Fiction.   7. Texas—Fiction.]   I. Title.
PZ7.A37719Par 2011
[Fic]—dc22
2010050900

Book design by Liz Tardiff

Feiwel and Friends logo designed by Filomena Tuosto

First Edition: 2011

10 9 8 7 6 5 4 3 2 1

macteenbooks.com

PARADISE

*This one goes out to all the small-town, rural route kids
who dream beyond the county line*

I

PARADISE
AND HIS SMOKIN'
SQUEEZEBOX

All it took to find Paradise was a five dollar bill and an ad in the *Thrifty Nickel*.

WANTED
Frontman for country rock band.
Good vocals. NO guitar players.
Auditions Thursday
CR 218, Cross the RR tracks,
1st left after peach grove
Dripping Springs Community

I was shocked, really, that the ad worked. For starters, cutting out all guitar players whittled the already-small field down to a nub. Most singers at some point in time had picked up a guitar. But Waylon, who considered himself anointed country-music royalty by right of his first name, never listened to reason. As a matter of fact, Waylon Slider didn't care what I thought as long as I showed up after school with my drumsticks and opened up my uncle L. V.'s airplane hangar to rehearse.

We'd been playing to the Piper Cub and the *Miss Molly Moonlight*

—painted on the nose of the old World War II bomber—for about an hour when Waylon put down his six-string and snatched up the want ads. His rusty, reddish brown hair mounded around his head in a tangled bird's nest of coarse curls. Sitting on his stool with a fistful of the *Thrifty Nickel*, Waylon looked like a pouty little Tom Sawyer in a time-out. He raked his top teeth across his bottom lip and pinched his bushy eyebrows together. He just couldn't make out why no one had answered the ad.

I twisted a bit on my stool, practicing a drumstick toss and backhanded catch. "You know, putting NO in all caps made us look like we had a bunch of insecure guitarists."

"Shut up, Paisley!" He rolled the *Thrifty Nickel* into a club and reared up. If I'd been a boy, I think he would have hit me. But he mumbled, "Blondes!" instead and sat back down. "You don't know anything about band management. Nobody cares what you think."

That last part was truer than he knew. But with Texapalooza in less than two months, my shot at playing on the same stage as some of the best drummers in the state seemed to be slipping away. The Waylon Slider Band needed a lead singer. So far, Waylon Slider had managed to screw that up.

A gust of March wind blasted the metal siding of the hangar walls like an echoing gong. Cal unplugged his lead guitar. Levi cased his bass.

I had left the tall sliding doors slightly open on the west side, the pasture side of the hangar. The evening sun hung just above the pine thicket in the distance, sending a rectangle of orange light between the doors and glinting off the chrome on my snare.

"Waylon." I stood up, tugging at the frayed edges of my cutoff shorts. "I've got to close up and be through the woods before it gets dark. There's always tomorrow. We'll find someone."

I reached for the tarp to hide my drums when the sunlight went black. Afraid I might have misjudged the time, I spun around. Faced the doors.

Filling the gap was a tall figure in a wide-brimmed hat. He stood with his feet apart and something slung over his shoulder like a saddlebag. Eclipsing the light, he looked like a cowboy cutout etched onto the setting sun.

Waylon jumped to his feet. "You're not here about the ad, are you?"

The boy didn't say anything. He ambled across the concrete floor with a bronc-busting swagger like he'd just gone eight seconds on Boom-Shocka-Locka. He pulled up in front of Waylon, cocked his head at Cal and Levi. The boy caught me in his crosshairs, homing in first on my denim cutoffs, then my boots.

I reached into my back pocket. Pulled out my drumsticks. I tossed one into my left hand and twirled the other by my side. Just to let him know I was more than eye candy and the role of band badass was taken.

He grinned, and when he did, the smooth center of his left cheek dimpled.

I dropped my drumstick. Slipping from *badass* to *dumb ass* in a heartbeat.

The boy watched it bounce and spin onto the floor. Then he gave Waylon a fist bump and said, "I sing some."

"Sweet. 'Cause we don't." Levi rolled the toothpick dangling off his lip from one corner of his mouth to the other. "*Some* will be an improvement."

Waylon's freckled face turned pink. It wrenched his gut that his voice slipped into a nasal honk when his nerves got the best of him. He grabbed his six-string by the neck. "You don't play guitar, right?"

The boy in the cowboy hat rubbed his hand over the strap of his bag. "Naw, man. Guitar's not my thing."

The flesh tone came back to Waylon's face. Since competition on guitar was all he seemed to care about, and Levi was willing to let a dog howl while we played as long as we got to play, it was up to me and Cal to check this guy out. I looked to Cal for some help, but he was bent over his spiral, hidden under his long hair, scribbling furiously.

I was going to have to ask the questions, and the light outside was growing dim. We were running out of time.

"Look," I started. I had never seen him before, so he was either new or went to one of the surrounding county schools. "Not to be rude. But I've got to lock up. So, who are you and where are you from?"

His black hat shaded his eyes, but I noticed that he had small gold loops in each earlobe. He wore a pearl snap shirt with the sleeves rolled up and cinched around his biceps. And the hem of his faded jeans was slit at the seams, probably to make it easier to fit over his boots.

"I'm Gabe." That dimple on his left cheek winked. "From Paradise."

Cal glanced up, shaking the hair away from his face.

Levi laughed and slapped both hands on his knees. "Well, dude, you're in for major disappointment, 'cause we ain't seen a chick in a coconut bra and a grass skirt since Halloween."

So much for professionalism.

"He means Texas," Waylon blurted. "Paradise, Texas, right?"

"Sure." The boy swung his bag from one shoulder to the other like he was toting a fifteen-pound sack of potatoes.

"Waylon." I tucked my sticks back into my pocket and threw the tarp over my drums. The *ting* of the cymbals rang through the hangar like the starting bell for the water-gun race at the Prosper County Fair. "Paradise has three minutes to prove he can sing."

"She's not joking," Waylon told him. "Sing something. Anything. Quick."

The last sliver of sunlight slipped into the hangar, reaching across the black-tarped drum set and touching the silver ring on my left hand.

With one knee slightly bent, the boy from Paradise tapped the heel of his boot against the floor three times—counting himself in. Then he growled out a husky Johnny Cash version of "This Little Light of Mine."

Before he could finish off the last "let it shine" and I could say, *You've got to be kidding,* Levi started clapping. He stopped long enough to take the toothpick out of his mouth and announce, "Good enough for me."

Waylon's face lit up. He raised his eyebrows at me and I gave in. The raspy, low tone of the boy's voice could add an edge to our sound. And he could stay on pitch. Even if he couldn't, Gabe from Paradise was our only hope.

Levi picked up his case and patted Waylon on the back on his way out. "If this whole band showcase thing doesn't work out, there's always Vacation Bible School down at the First Baptist

Church." Then he squeezed his big frame between the double doors, bumping his butt against one of them to open it a little wider.

Cal shoved his spiral between the books and the skateboard in his backpack. He heaved it over his shoulder, picked up his guitar case. He walked over to Gabe and shook his hand. Gabe's smooth, tan forearm flexed, making Cal's thin arm look as fragile as a sparrow's leg.

"Later, Cal," I called as he headed through the doors to catch his ride with Levi.

"Looks like you're in, man," Waylon said.

Gabe shook Waylon's freckled hand. Then he reached out to me. The strap on his black shoulder bag slid down to his elbow.

"You're losing your man purse." I folded my arms at my waist and smiled. I'd never seen a big ol' stud cowboy with a murse. "Most of the guys around here carry their books in a backpack."

He grabbed the strap and eased the bag onto the floor, staring at the top of my blond spikes. "And do most girl drummers Marine-cut their hair and wear purity rings?"

I could've speared him with one of my drumsticks. My hair was *not* that short.

Waylon wedged between us.

"Don't mind Paisley," he said, glaring at me. "She gets antsy when it starts to get dark. She has to get home. Her uncle lets us use this place, but her mother doesn't know she's in the band."

The band. I settled down and blew off his stripped-down assessment of my appearance. I deserved it. Uncle L. V. always warned me not to let my mouth get a jump on my judgment. Besides, I had to think about the band.

"So, Paradise," I began.

His shirt hugged his broad shoulders as he knelt beside his bag, almost making a murse manly. He was a hot mess, probably used to girls wilting from the heat off his ego.

"You sing and you said guitar's not your thing. What is? Fiddle? Keyboard?"

He pulled something from his bag.

His back was to me, but not to Waylon's. A whitewash of horror covered Waylon as the blood drained from his face.

Gabe stood up, strapping himself into a red three-row button accordion.

Paradise played squeezebox.

Waylon all but slumped to his knees like some weary nomad finding a pool in the desert only to realize it was a mirage.

I went ahead and stated the obvious. "Well, that's unexpected."

"No way is that going to work." Waylon shook his head. "We're not a freakin' polka band."

Despite the fact that he struggled with singing and had a history of hyperventilating, Waylon Slider maintained a protective vision of the coolness of his own band. A vision built on his bluegrass bloodline and screaming twelve-year-olds at the county fair.

"This is what I play." Paradise unstrapped the accordion and slipped it back into the bag. "And I don't sing with people who don't get it."

I didn't know of anything musically that Waylon didn't get. And Paradise's comment seemed to irk him; Waylon's blood boiled back into his face. He could be a hot-tempered imp, holding his breath until he got his way.

But no amount of breath-holding was going to change the fact that if we wanted him to sing, Paradise was going to play squeezebox.

"It's just an accordion, Waylon." I tried to coax him as Paradise stood there in his snug jeans and smug attitude. "Think Charles Gillingham with the Counting Crows or Michael Stipe with R.E.M."

Paradise raised his chin up and for the first time, I got a good look at his eyes—deep pine green with gold flecks that mirrored his earrings.

"Don't look so surprised." I strolled past him.

Through the hangar doors, I could see the gray twilight deepening to a dark purple. Rich sunsets were one of the few advantages to being stuck on the less prosperous end of Prosper County and isolated miles outside of the town of Big Wells. I headed out with Waylon and Paradise behind me. "We might be just a hick high school band"—I slid the heavy doors together and padlocked them—"but make no mistake, we know our music. Waylon's greatgranddaddy played bluegrass with Flatt and Scruggs, and he's been backporch picking since he could walk. Be here next Monday," I told Paradise. "And be sure you can play that thing."

I threw my leg over the four-wheeler and turned it on. It sputtered and shook like an old truck on a cold morning. With my drumsticks in my back pocket, I zipped my hoodie and hit the throttle—tearing out across the pasture and into the woods. I didn't care if he blew on a jug. Everybody has a gift, and if his was pumping an accordion, so be it. Finding Paradise meant we finally had a lead singer and could enter the amateur band contest at Texapalooza. All the bigwigs from Austin to Nashville would be there.

Racing through the piney woods on an old deer run, I leaned low over the handlebars—the damp wind chilling my face and legs. The four-wheeler stalled just as I broke through the thicket into the back pasture. I hit the starter twice and revved the motor. Gassy fumes hung in the dank night air. I squeezed the accelerator hard, speeding along the fence row to our gate. Just to the side of the cattle guard, a round hay bale that Mother had painted with the pink face of the Easter Bunny watched me like some sick funhouse clown.

I sped home. Down the driveway. To our yellow frame house at the end of the blacktop.

I was finally going to get my chance to drum my way out of Dripping Springs and far beyond Prosper County. Me. Running down my own dream. All I had left to do was keep my mother from setting up a roadblock.

A HAT LIKE THAT

You can show up in boots, be shrink-wrapped in denim
Karaoke some with Willie and Hank
But you'll need skills in the saddle, dude
If you're gonna wear a hat like that.

Your Stetson's blocking the sun, leavin' me in the
    shadow
But I ain't gonna stay here for long
This guitar's my friend, the girls love real thunder
I'm no poser, I'm where it's at
So you'd better own some land, stock some cattle
If you're gonna wear a hat like that.

I can tell you like black, into symbols
Bet you jam to Jennings and Cash
But they kicked out the lights, shot up a finger
Ain't nothin' symbolic about that
So you'd better find a bull, beat eight seconds
If you're gonna wear a hat like that.

I don't begrudge you a lid, maybe you need one
Not everyone can grow rock star hair
But if you're jackin' an image to hide a weakness
You're really not changin' your stats
Wrestle a steer, dude, and get to ropin'
If you're gonna wear a hat like that.

2

DREAMS DEFERRED

I caught the screen door just before it slammed behind me. Bunnies, some in fancy velvet coats and some in overalls, gawked at me as I slipped into the kitchen. We were a few weeks away from Easter, and Mother was a seasonal decorator.

My older sister Lacey stood with her arms out to her sides and stared vacantly through the kitchen window while Mother hot-glued the last of the pink rhinestones on her wide belt. Despite the fact that it was the spring of Lacey's senior year, Mother festooned Lacey in sparkles and Spandex. With her ruffled white blouse and tight white jeans squeezing her fat rolls, Lacey looked like the un-happy puppet bride of the Michelin Man.

I ladled a bowl of steamy chicken and dumplings and sat down at the table by my dad. He'd been practicing with the church softball team and had red dirt stains on his T-shirt. "What's her costume for this time?" I asked.

Mother forced a princess tiara onto a pink cowboy hat and placed it on Lacey's head. "It's an outfit, Paisley. An outfit your sister will wear when she has the honor of singing at the rodeo next week."

Then she sighed a haggard breath like I just wore her out every time I opened my mouth. "Anyhoo, it's not a costume. A costume is that gosh-awful, unflattering man-suit you call a marching band uniform."

I shoved a fat dumpling in my mouth. Mother had long ago given up the fight with me and choir and sequined outfits. She hated the fact that I chose to twirl drumsticks instead of a baton, and the only reason she tolerated my being in the school band was because I had to have a fine arts credit. Mother would certainly have a cow if she knew I played drums in the Waylon Slider Band.

Lacey took off the hat. "This is mashing my hair down," she complained.

Honestly, nothing could mash Lacey's hair down. She'd hot-rolled, backcombed, teased, and plastered her thick blond curls into a warrior-like helmet. But I couldn't blame her for trying to come up with an excuse not to wear that phony pageant-girl hat.

I tried to help her. "Looks better without the hat."

Mother kept her back to me and bobby-pinned the hat to Lacey's hair. They were almost mirror images of each other, wide in the hips and meringue-high hairdos. "You were too late getting home today, Paisley. If you want to continue to work for L. V., then you better be home before dark."

I scooped up another dumpling. Somehow, I'd managed to convince my mother that I cleaned her brother's house every day after school. She always said Uncle L. V. and I were cut from the same cloth, and she knew that I liked being around him. But she'd pluck that privilege quicker than spit if I interfered with her plans for Lacey or if she got wind that I used L. V.'s old drum set to rehearse with the band. Mother held fast to her own notions about our futures. She just couldn't seem to let go of her fear that Lacey and I would end up pregnant in high school and stuck in Prosper County. Just like her.

"Your mother sure did miss her calling." Dad took a big bite of buttery cornbread then crumbled the rest into his bowl of dumplings with one hand. He ran his other hand under the table and jerked the drumsticks out of my back pocket.

I froze. Spoon in midair.

Dad tucked the sticks under my leg.

"Honey, I think you could've had one of them cooking-and-decorating shows on TV. *Cooking and Crafts with Diane Tillery*," he said, never missing a beat.

I got rhythm from him.

"Coulda, woulda, shoulda," Mother mumbled with a mouthful of bobby pins.

I eased the drumsticks under my hoodie.

Dad knew about the band. I was pretty sure. Somehow the four-wheeler was gassed up every afternoon. But he never mentioned it. In my house, being tight-lipped equaled honesty. No need to mention. No need to lie. No need to send Mother into a tailspin.

Lacey, in her pink-and-white cowgirl getup, grabbed her neck and started some coughing, throat-clearing drama.

"I—I—I—I," Lacey barked like a sick sheep, "ne—ed to rest my vo—oice."

Mother tripped over her own feet rushing to the sink to fill a glass of water. She held it to Lacey's lips. Lacey took a couple of sips, fanning herself the whole time.

"Lacey's got to rest her voice," Mother announced as if Dad and I should put our dinner on pause for a moment of silence.

Dad picked up a ceramic bunny shaker and peppered his dumplings. I heard Lacey cough and hack her way down the hall to her bedroom.

"Good golly golly! I hope she's a hundred percent by rodeo time." Mother sorted rhinestones and bobby pins and sequins into the tiny compartments of her toolbox. "You know Reba McEntire got her big break singing at a rodeo."

But I bet Reba actually wanted to sing. I wasn't so sure about Lacey.

Mother snickered then shook both her hands in the air like she'd made some life-changing discovery. "Oh, oh, oh and get this one: When I signed Lacey up, I heard them talking about trying to get that white-trash Waylon Slider to play some a-coustic version of 'The Star-Spangled Banner' on a guitar."

The hair on my arms went stiff as porcupine quills.

"I said right quick," Mother quoted herself, "'I don't think so, Scooter. You can just back up off that. Everybody knows that song don't mean nothing without the words. What are people gonna do? Put their hands over their hearts and hum?'" She threw her head back and cackled. "They said that boy was getting some band together to go play at that Texapa-*loser* thing in Austin."

The comforting smell of chicken broth filling the kitchen suddenly soured. With that comment, she'd just slammed the lid on any fantasy I had about having a come-to-Jesus meeting with her and being honest about my musical intentions. Mother held a permanent grudge against Waylon and his family because they were actually a musically gifted bunch. For years, the Sliders won every county-fair talent competition with their banjo-picking bluegrass, and they ruled our annual church Christmas program. Mother had to work overtime to secure Lacey a part as a humming angel.

"Can you imagine?" she continued. "I don't care who his daddy is. A redneck high school runt thinking he can go from the Big Wells's marching band straight to an Austin grandstand!" With that, Mother wound the cord around her glue gun, shoved it in her toolbox, and snapped it shut. "He thinks he can just advance to go and move his little shoe around the board and skip on by everybody else."

I thought about Paradise and his red accordion. She'd absolutely have a runaway fit with that information. But I kept quiet. A four-wheel drive and a winch couldn't pull that out of me. I washed down her slam on Waylon and the band with a gulp of sweet tea, then kissed Dad on his forehead. I had to get out of the room before I defended Waylon and gave my mother a reason to snoop. "I'm going to check on Lacey."

Mother chimed, "Don't bother her with a bunch of questions, Paisley. She's got to rest. There's a lot riding on that rodeo performance."

I kept my arm close, pressing the drumsticks tight against my stomach. "I understand," I told her. "I understand." I knew something about having a lot riding on a performance. Texapalooza was one combination on the lock that released me from Prosper County.

Lacey lay on her stomach picking at the little pink balls of chenille on her bedspread with her French-manicured nails. Her silver abstinence ring, the one Mother gave her that matched mine, lay among a few pennies on her nightstand. "*Really* good kisser." She giggled into her cell phone. "Oh, gotta go." She flipped the phone shut.

I sat down among a menagerie of stuffed animals piled on a chair. "That coughing thing was one of your better performances."

Lacey heaved herself off the bed and stood in front of her dressing table—an antique chest topped with a tri-fold salon mirror, which Mother bought at the beauty supply. "You've got to help me, Paisley. I'm desperate. I just might die." Lacey jabbed at her hair with the pointy end of a teasing comb. "I ain't wearin' that pink hat."

"Just tell her you're not going to wear it."

"Right, and you can tell her about the band." Lacey slapped the comb down and popped open a tackle box full of makeup. She click-clacked eye shadows and blushes around, finally pulling out a tube of concealer. "You know we can't just *tell* Drill Sergeant Diane anything."

"Maybe you could forget the hat, leave it at home."

Lacey stopped dabbing the concealer under her eyes. "*Psshhhhh!*" She spewed like the air brake on an eighteen-wheeler.

I understood. We'd never had any luck leaving stuff behind. Mother kept a plastic storage box full of costumes and a karaoke machine in the Suburban at all times. She'd doll Lacey up and have her throw down a performance at a moment's notice. I felt bad for Lacey. I might be hindered from doing what I loved, but at least I wasn't made to do something I hated.

I wanted Lacey to put a stop to it.

"You're a senior, Lacey. Two months away from graduation.

Seems like a good time to bring an end to singing if you don't want to do it anymore."

"Not yet, Paisley." Lacey lifted up the bottom compartment of her tackle box and pulled out an envelope. "I should've thrown a conniption a long time ago like you did when she put us in prairie skirts and tried to pitch us as the modern-day Mary and Laura Ingalls. But I didn't. And I've paid and paid for it ever since." Lacey handed me the envelope. Her face lit up and she got all giddy with a huge grin. "Look at this."

Inside was a glossy pamphlet with a shiny-haired group of girls on the cover: GLAMOUR BEAUTY COLLEGE. I opened the pamphlet. *Get started on a beautiful career.*

"I thought you were going to Prosper County Community College in the fall?"

"I can do that too." She beamed. For the first time, I saw real passion in her eyes. Lacey had a dream, and it sure wasn't singing. "I could get a business degree *and* go to beauty school. Have my own salon! A full-service spa with massages and pedicure chairs!" She grabbed me by my shoulders and parked me in the chair in front of the mirror.

All Lacey had ever wanted was to do hair and makeup. But Mother had big plans for her to sing in college. I wondered how Lacey was planning on scooting around that. "What about the Singing Eagles?"

Lacey gently brushed out my spikes and practiced styling my short hair into more of a pixie. "I'll try out for the group," she said. "But I won't make it. Get real, Paisley! You know I'm not that good." Lacey pulled two little pieces of hair in front of my ears. "Mother will just have to give up on my singing then."

Lacey continued to brush and comb and curl and tuck my hair. It was what she loved to do. She seemed to have zero problem duping our mother to get what she wanted, which from where I sat looked a lot like more makeup and hair accessories. We both had our dreams all right. We just had different ways of chasing them down.

I took my drumsticks out from under my hoodie. The tips were worn down smooth and it was almost time for new ones. I hated hiding my love for the drums and the band. But I hated even more the thought of losing them both. I rubbed the worn wood between my fingers. The sound of Mother cleaning the kitchen, clanking pots and pans, played in my head like distant war drums.

Lacey clipped a blue rhinestone-flower barrette into my hair.

"Not bad," I told her.

"It softens your look and makes your blue eyes pop," she said. Then she came at me pumping a tube of lip gloss.

If she could hold out long enough, Lacey could probably ease our mother into giving up on the singing career and getting behind the cosmetology.

I'd never get that kind of support. *Drums are for boys. Bands are full of pot smokers and slackers,* she'd declared the day I broke free from her pageant prison. *There's a big world out there, Paisley. I'm not going to let you screw up your life by hanging out with the wrong crowd. Mark my words. I'll fall prostrate over the tracks to stop that hell train.*

So I'd hide my drumsticks and my dream as long as necessary. And come Monday afternoon, I would be on the other side of the pine thicket in Uncle L. V.'s airplane hangar driving the beat for the Waylon Slider Band.

3

BACKDOOR BAD BOY

Being a bachelor and retired military man, Uncle L. V. kept his house as tidy and clutter free as a school library. All I had to do was unload the dishwasher, dust what little furniture he had, and run a damp mop over the kitchen and den floors. That way my mother couldn't make him out to be a liar if she found out about the band rehearsing in his hangar. Technically, I was cleaning.

What he lacked in furniture, L. V. made up for in audio equipment. He had the old frame farmhouse wired with surround sound and a sweet subwoofer that shook the leaves on the pecan trees outside. He kept his stereo loaded with vintage Southern rock— Skynyrd, Allman Brothers, 38 Special. The mop and I tore it up every afternoon.

I was grooving across the hardwood. Sliding on the soles of my worn-down boots. Shaking it with the mop. Playing a little air guitar. All-out singing "Sweet Home Alabama." Then I twisted around, thought I'd try dropping it low. But the only thing I dropped was the mop.

I spun around and came face-to-face with Paradise. Earrings, hat, and all. I jumped a foot high and screamed. The boy stood right in front of me. Straight out of nowhere. Uninvited. Close enough to slap.

My heart raced. "What are you doing in here?" I asked him between breaths.

"I said 'Paisley,'" he drawled in his honeyed bass, "three, maybe four times." He kept a straight face as if I actually believed it. Then he reached down, picked up the mop. I hadn't noticed that my denim cutoffs had wiggled lower and my shirt had ridden up. Paradise pointed the mop handle at my belly button. "*You* didn't answer." His left cheek dimpled. "So I just decided to watch the show."

My face burned red-hot. "Show's over." I jerked the mop away from him. "The band meets in the hangar, not in the house."

"Nobody was in the hangar." Paradise took off his hat and held it by the crown against his thigh. His dark, wavy hair shined like black silk and twisted into soft ringlets at the top of his shirt collar. His wide hand covered the hat's crown. "The back door was open. I wasn't trying to scare you."

"Well, you didn't. And you've got a loose definition of *open*." I marched toward the laundry room, gripping the mop handle in my sweaty hand. "*Unlocked* and *open* aren't the same."

Paradise snickered a little but never looked my way. He propped his boot on the fireplace hearth and hung his hat on his knee. He seemed smitten with one of L. V.'s few decorative items—a collection of straw hats woven in alternating rings of black and white displayed on the mantel.

"What sort of work does your uncle do?" he asked.

"He flies transport helicopters, taking workers from Houston to offshore drilling rigs." I stood by the door. Ready to head to the hangar. Ready to get behind my drums.

Paradise gently placed one of the hats on his head.

"Put that right back where you got it. My uncle's particular about his stuff, and we need to go practice."

Paradise ignored me. He put the one hat back down and picked up another. This one had little black-and-white woven triangle shapes in addition to the rings.

"Colombian cowboy hats." He ran his fingers across the brim then put it back in line with the others. "Did your uncle live in Colombia or does he just collect hats?"

"He lived somewhere in South America after the first Gulf War, I think." The pounding in my chest had softened. I was ready to go rehearse, but Paradise's interest in the hats got the better of me. L. V. was as tight-lipped about his South American activities as I was about the band. "You sure those are Colombian?"

"No doubt."

He took his own hat off his knee and strutted beside me, staring at my fingers tapping on the doorknob. My nervous drummer's habit. Paradise reached for my hand and rubbed his thumb across the inscription on my ring.

He read the words etched into the silver. "'One life, one love.'" Then he leaned against the doorframe and cleared his voice. "How's that working for you?"

"Like a charm," I blurted. "Works like a charm." I didn't even know what I was saying, but I knew that I'd suffocate if I had to share the same air with him anymore. "Works great."

"Maybe it's just never been tested," he said.

I tried not to look at him and pushed open the door. The bright sunshine hit me like a camera flash.

Paradise followed me outside and took in a deep breath. His chest swelled, and I thought the snaps on his plaid shirt might pop. He caught me staring at him, the gold flecks in his green eyes twinkling in the sun. "Breathe, Paisley," he whispered. "Life's short."

The spring smell of wild honeysuckle blooming along the fence row floated in the afternoon breeze.

I tried to just focus on the band. But it was no use. I was all caught up in a dizzying swirl of sweet honeysuckle and back-door bad boy. I had to breathe to keep from fainting.

An old Ford Bronco, restored with a shiny coat of baby blue paint, was parked on the grassy area between the house and the hangar.

I came to my senses.

"That yours?" I giggled at the nursery color.

Paradise didn't answer. He just reached into the backseat and pulled out his murse.

The buzz of a plane coming in the distance filled the awkward silence. Over acres of farmland and pine thickets, L. V.'s red Piper Cub sailed like a cardinal against the sapphire sky.

I waved both arms above my head. L. V. circled his house and rocked his wings at me before landing on the closely shredded strip in his back pasture.

"He doesn't drive back and forth to Houston?" Paradise asked.

"Nope. He says the interstate is too dangerous, and the day he can't fly is the day we can bury him in a pine box in that peach orchard." I pointed to the grove on the other side of L. V.'s house.

Paradise watched the plane glide low over the treetops and settle safely onto the grassy runway. He shook his head and grimaced as if L. V.'s pasture landing was like playing Russian roulette. Spin the barrel. Pull the trigger. Odds were that sooner or later he'd lose. "Seems like a risky way to get back and forth to a job."

I laughed. *Risky* wasn't in L. V.'s vocabulary, and Paradise just might be afraid to fly. "An earring-wearing, murse-carrying accordion player with a baby blue ride and a fear of flying." I skipped by him on my way to the hangar and yelled out, "How's *that* working for you?"

The bright yellow sunlight had turned to marigold in the late afternoon. Paradise stood with his hands on hips, his murse over his shoulder, and all the self-confidence in the world.

Other than taking care of business at school, all I ever thought about was rehearsing, getting to Texapalooza, maybe going to Nashville after high school and college, and drumming professionally. That was the only interest I ever had, ever thought about.

Until now.

4

STRIKE UP THE BAND

The lights were on inside the hangar. *Miss Molly Moonlight*, shining on the nose of the B-25 bomber, leaned on a crescent moon in all her buxom 1940s glory.

I paused in the doorway.

Cal sat in a lawn chair tuning his black Gibson Les Paul. Last year, when he turned sixteen, Cal took his savings from mowing lawns and spent every last dime on the guitar instead of a car.

Levi, with his hands tucked behind the bib of his overalls, bobbed his head as Waylon warmed up on a banjo. Waylon and I had spent too much of our childhood in Sunday school together to actually like each other, but God knows I loved to watch him play. He could play anything with strings and plucked the banjo in a blur; no one had faster fingers than Waylon's.

A shadow fell in front of me. Paradise put his hand on my shoulder.

"You going to watch or play?" He pointed to the tarp at the back of the hangar as if I didn't know where my own drums were. "Time to rock and roll." Then he blew past me, straight to the boys.

I pulled the tarp off my drums, listening as Waylon instructed Paradise on our playlist and plans.

"We open with Guns N' Roses." Waylon handed Paradise one of his homemade band handbooks and pointed to a list on the first page. "Cal can play the intro and solo to 'Sweet Child O'Mine' as good as Slash and everyone recognizes the song. It'll get the crowd warmed up. Then we speed up the tempo, probably with Brooks and Dunn or something Texas like Pat Green." He chewed on his bottom lip for a minute and said, "You're only going to sing at first. No accordion."

I dropped my head. *Here we go again,* I thought. *Waylon with his controlling ways is going to screw up and lose another lead singer.*

Paradise hung his thumbs in his front pockets and raised his chin, glaring at Waylon.

"Just listen." Waylon flipped a couple pages in the notebook. From where I stood, I could see some musical notes drawn among song lyrics. "This is our stuff. Cal's written some. I've written some. I added the notes for your accordion." Waylon glanced up at Paradise. "If you're any good on it."

Cal and Levi didn't flinch when Waylon brought up the accordion. He must've given them a heads-up over the weekend.

I sat down on my stool and started pumping the bass drum. *Thump. Thump. Thump.* Waylon would yap on about the band and skill and musical history. At some point, we had to shut up and play. For me, that point had come.

Cal, in his checkered Vans, weaved in front of me rocking some psychedelic guitar riff. I drummed the snare then rolled from crash to ride, and we were on. Full tilt.

Levi pulled his bass strap over his shoulder.

Waylon grabbed his guitar. "On two, Paisley."

I crossed my drumsticks above my head and hit them twice. Cal plowed into the intro for "Sweet Child O'Mine."

Dropping Waylon's homemade band manual on the floor, Paradise took his place in front of the four of us. He hit his vocal. Right on cue. Almost like a serenade. "She's got a smile . . ."

I slowed the backbeat, bringing the song down to a rocking lullaby that suited his deep voice. Levi hitched his bass to the beat. With Waylon strumming his acoustic guitar and Cal improvising on lead, the country-rock sound of the Waylon Slider Band took off.

Sometimes when I played, I got the urge to tear it up, just pound away like I was running across the pasture racing for home. But at the moment, like a kid swinging on a summer afternoon, I closed my eyes and rode the rhythm.

Paradise all but cooed the last "sweet love of mine."

"Dude, that was sexy," Levi blurted. He had his trucker hat on backward. "You gonna get some digits with that joint."

Paradise leaned down and pulled his accordion from his murse. "I sang." He stared at Waylon. "Now I play."

He never gave Waylon a chance to argue. Paradise strapped himself into his red accordion and ran his fingers over the buttons as if each one were as white-hot as the tip end of a lit match. He drew the center bellows apart, drawing out a sweeping organlike sound.

"Well, if you don't kill 'em with the accordion"—Levi stared at the cinched sleeves hugging Paradise's biceps—"you can always bring out the guns."

Waylon put down his guitar and huffed. "We're not a circus act."

"You see somebody clowning?" Paradise dared Waylon to utter a negative word about the accordion.

Levi knew when to shut up. Cal fidgeted with his amp.

"Can we play, please?" I never got up from my stool. Stroking Waylon's temperamental side was a task I'd grown accustomed to. A happy, unstressed Waylon meant a definite trip to Texapalooza. A happy Paradise meant we actually could be in the band competition once we got there. I wasn't about to let either of their egos ruin my chance at getting on that stage.

I counted us in on four. Cal hit the opening melody to one of Waylon's songs. He understood that the way to work Waylon was to prop up Waylon's music.

Levi linked up his bass. Waylon grabbed the neck of his blues guitar, drawing out a moaning underwater sound, showing off like he was freakin' B. B. King or something.

Paradise flicked Waylon's notebook open with the toe of his boot. His back was to me, and I couldn't help but notice how he filled out his jeans. Paradise couldn't have slipped a greased ruler in either back pocket. I stumbled over a beat. Levi kept it going with his bass and smiled at me.

At first, Paradise pulled and pushed the accordion just on the downbeats—almost like an accent. Then he seemed to settle into the bluesy groove of Waylon's song. He shifted sideways slightly and I could see that his eyes were closed. His fingers began to race across the buttons as he pumped the accordion like a giant red lung, panting with the music.

Waylon and Cal backed off their runs and gave Paradise a solo, a chance to prove what he could do. His knees were slightly bent and Paradise threw his whole body into the work of playing the accordion. Fanning the accordion open. Pushing the bellows together. Making it wave in and out. Swaying like a cowboy version of a New Orleans jazz star.

Paradise could play. That was for sure.

Waylon glanced at me with the look of a surprised little boy who'd just been given the keys to a shiny new pickup. I knew what he was thinking. No other band would have a stud accordion player. With Paradise and his smoking squeezebox, the Waylon Slider Band had just become unique.

And he could sing. He made Waylon's lyrics his own and threw a couple vocal hiccups in on the chorus, bouncing his shoulders and teasing with every hip-hip.

When we finished, Levi took his trucker hat off and rubbed his closely shaved head. "Dude, you're like Buddy Holly or something. That hip-hip hiccup stuff is crazy."

Crazy didn't begin to describe it. Girls were going to go nuts.

Levi kept rubbing his head like he had something on his mind.

"I wasn't going to say anything 'cause we didn't have a singer." Levi didn't look at Waylon. "But, I think I've got us a gig."

Paradise spun around on the heels of his boots. I gripped my sticks. Our first gig.

"Where might that be?" Waylon had his hands on his hips, acting half offended that he didn't know about it.

"Well." Levi patted his thick overalled belly. "The Tucker Barn."

"One of your barn parties?" I fell onto my stool. Tucker Barn parties were notorious for such activities as Everclear-soaked watermelons, cow tipping, and snipe hunting. "We'd have to play behind chicken wire to keep from getting assaulted."

"You wouldn't know that from experience now, would ya?" Levi pressed his lips together and swallowed like he'd just eaten a roach. He took no pleasure in chiding me.

But he was right. I'd never even been in the Tucker Barn. Mother would homeschool me sure as daylight if I even asked to go.

"My big brother's got a band coming from over in Jessup County." Levi looked around at each of us. "I checked. They said we could use their equipment for a few songs while they take a break."

Cal nodded and Paradise agreed. "I'll bring my own equipment," he said with his arm resting on his accordion.

Waylon shifted his weight, locking eyes with Levi.

Levi looked away, staring at the frets on his bass guitar.

Paradise's jaw tightened and twitched. He seemed to take Waylon's and Levi's sudden silence personally. He put his hands on his hips—the accordion strapped to him like a bullet bandolier. "You people don't really want to play in a band." Paradise reached for his murse. "You only want to say you're in one."

But this time, Paradise had it all wrong.

"Not true," I said. "They're not worried about you or your accordion." I rolled my sticks back and forth across the tops of my legs until they felt hot. "It's me, isn't it?"

Waylon almost looked apologetic. "We've got to have a drummer."

"The Waylon Slider Band has a drummer. The same one it's had from the start." I stood up with my sticks in my fist.

"Paisley, your mother's not going to let you within ten miles of the Tucker Barn."

"That's not your problem, Waylon." I stepped out from behind my drums, my boots clapping across the concrete. If Waylon Slider was going to tell me I couldn't play, he'd have to tell it within punching range. "Where the band plays, I play. I'm not just your rehearsal drummer."

Levi started laughing. "God, Paisley. No one's gonna confuse you with a rehearsal drummer. But if we're gonna do this thing, you gotta promise to be there." Then Levi drew in a deep breath as if he knew what kind of underhanded maneuvering it would take. "Regardless."

"And if you blow this and get caught," Waylon kicked in, "you'll sure enough be out for Austin. And"—he rolled his mouth around and finally mumbled out—"we need you the most at Texapalooza."

Levi reached his big arm around my waist and pulled me away from Waylon. "You're the best drummer in these parts."

Like Lacey, Levi was a senior and had treated me like his baby sister ever since I joined the school band in junior high. "If you say you'll be there, we know you'll show." Then he added, "Good Lord knows your sister always manages to show up."

"Done deal, then," Paradise said.

Cal sat in a lawn chair, his long hair falling like a curtain over the spiral in his lap. But he held his pencil up for a quick second, just long enough to let us know he was in.

"Saturday night. After the rodeo." Levi hit me with a soft fist bump.

"No problem," I lied. Truth was—I had no earthly idea how I was going to pull off getting to and from Levi Tucker's barn party, but that was just logistics.

BAPTIZED BY FIRE

I kissed her in first grade
>Gave her my lemonade
>Said, "Girl, will you marry me?"
But she kicked dirt on my new Vans
>Laughed at my big plans
>Forced me to learn the hard way
She left me baptized by fire reaching out for
  a dream.

Her momma tried hard to keep her home
>Set up some orange cones
>Said, "Girl, keep it between the lines"
But she hung a left off the straight and narrow
>All wing, no halo
>Nothing to slow the pace
She'll be baptized by fire on the road to her dream.

Someday this trip will end
>She'll really need a friend
>I'll say, "Girl, it's been a long time."

Since you've come around to notice me
        Strumming patiently
        I've been here all along
We've both been baptized by fire chasing down a dream.

5

RODEO

A cloud of red dirt dusted the Prosper County Rodeo Arena like a soft sifting of chili powder. Gusts of wind picked up the grassy smell of manure in the pens and the greasy scent of fried food from the concession stands—carrying both into the crowded arena. My spot on the eighth row in the bleachers was a little like standing behind a horse while eating a corny dog.

Dad stuck his bag of popcorn under my nose. "Want some?"

I shook my head, hoping Lacey would sing soon and get this show on the road. I didn't want to go to the Tucker Barn smelling like a feedlot. But more than that, Lacey's performing set me on edge. She didn't want to sing. She wanted to be a hairstylist and makeup artist. That lack of interest in singing had become all too apparent lately in her lackluster delivery. I glanced around the arena. Denim and boots everywhere. A lot of old-time veterans with military pins on their caps. This was definitely not the place to blow the national anthem.

"Your mother said you and Lacey were headed out after her performance," Dad said, picking around in his popcorn sack.

"Yep." I looked away, tapping my fingertips against the metal bleacher seat.

Lacey had laughed when I asked if I could ride with her to the Tucker Barn, but she didn't say no. She walked straight into the kitchen and told Mother we were going to the late movie after the rodeo and wouldn't be home until after midnight. Mother bought the lie. No questions asked. When it came to Lacey, she just believed what she wanted to believe.

Dad was different.

"Well, Paisley." Dad leaned back on the bleacher row. He was younger than most dads, and he kept his hair longer too, like a gladiator in an epic movie. "Sometimes you can get yourself in a movie or whatever that's no good. Maybe realize you made a bad choice."

I tugged the little twigs of hair at the base of my neck. I'd have to turn around to see his face, so I just stared hard at the steer wranglers sitting high on their horses and spinning their lassoes above their heads and watched Mother pace on the walkway at the bottom of the bleachers, occasionally sighting in her video camera on the area around the chutes.

Dad rubbed my back. "I'll tell you like I told Lacey when she was sixteen and starting to go out some. I'll always come get you girls. No matter where. No matter why." He stopped rubbing and sat back up. "Just because you make a bad choice doesn't mean you have to stay there and waller in it. I guess what I'm trying to say is I've got your back."

I cringed at his slang, but regardless, Dad was my hero.

George Strait blared from the loudspeakers. The girls from Big Bubba's Pizza rode into the arena in the bed of a fire engine red Chevrolet truck. The girls were at least college age and seemed experienced in the dancing department. They held up signs and wore skimpy white tank tops emblazoned with Big Bubba's slogan: THE BEST

PIECE IN TOWN. They wiggled and bounced in the back of that truck, circling the arena several times, throwing T-shirts into the crowd.

Mother stopped her pacing and hollered back at Dad and me. "That's so tacky!" Mother had on her favorite blue jeans, the pair with the yellow rhinestone star on the back pocket. The jeans clung to her like Spandex bicycle pants and stacked around her ankles, showing off her lemon yellow satin evening shoes.

When the truck came back around with the Best Piece in Town girls, Mother kissed her index finger and pointed to the Lord above—her idea of being a Christian witness. But when the girls looked up, all they saw was arena roof so they went right back to T-shirt tossing.

Dad zinged Mother with popcorn. He threw one piece, and it landed on the yellow star and bounced off.

"Watch this," he said, landing another.

Mother turned around, brushing her backside.

Dad winked at her. "Nice target, honey."

She pinched her lips together like she was trying not to smile.

I laughed. Dad took pride in hitting where he aimed. Nerve damage cost him a major-league pitching career, but he continued to throw even if it was just popcorn or horse apples or church league softball. And no matter how annoyed we all got with Mother, he knew the code to softening her up.

"Ladies and gentlemen," the announcer called to everyone. "Direct your attention to the arena and welcome four-time state champion barrel racer, the Angel from Amarillo, the Cowgirl on Comet, Miss Rodeo Texas, Jenny Boggs."

From the gate at the end of the arena, Miss Rodeo Texas shot out on a horse as dark as midnight. Her black silk shirt shimmered in the lights and the rhinestones on the crown attached to her black hat sparkled like real diamonds. She swept round the arena like a shooting star, holding the reins with one hand and carrying the American flag with the other. Under a center spotlight, she pulled the horse to a sudden stop. The horse reared up on its hind legs, first to one side of the audience then to the other.

Dad and I and the rest of the crowd jumped to our feet clapping and whooping. I watched the face of Miss Rodeo Texas. I wanted that smile, the ear-to-ear grin of a girl living her dream.

Now that the band had found Paradise, by my count, I was less than two months away from wearing that grin.

"Now for your national anthem," the announcer called.

Everyone stood in complete silence. The place was packed. Miss Rodeo Texas stayed in the center of the arena—high on her horse, holding the flag in her left hand and her right pressed against her heart.

Lacey stood at the gate near the bull chutes in her pink and white cowgirl costume. The heels of her Pepto-Bismol pink boots sunk in the red dirt, and she had the pink cowboy hat with the fake princess crown pulled low. I couldn't see her eyes. Her blond corkscrew curls poofed under the hat like one of those Halloween masks with the hair attached. When the recording of "The Star-Spangled Banner" started, Lacey didn't. The bawling from the steers in the pens behind her must've thrown her off. She tried to pick up with "by the dawn's early light," but she started off-key. Two twin toddlers, sitting a few rows back, cried when she hit the first high note. Lacey continued to sing off-key and out of touch with the recorded melody.

Mother quit videoing. She nervously grabbed at the railing in front of her, twisting her hand around the top bar. Then she slapped at the bar in time with the recording. She waved the video camera high in the air with her other hand, trying to get Lacey's attention. Even if Lacey could've seen through her hair to get on the beat with Mother, she was too deep in the song to turn back.

With my hand already crossing my heart, I prayed for Lacey that somehow the end of the song would be better than the beginning. The last note was all people ever really remembered anyway.

But Lacey's voice fluttered on every word like the mad beating wings of a butterfly in a jar. I spotted a little boy across the arena flapping his arms. As she sang the emotional run of the song, "Oh-oh say does that star-spangled ba-a-ner-er yet wa-ve," she pounded her fist against her white jeans, keeping time. When she finally squawked her way to the highest note of "free," the feedback between the microphone and speakers could've pierced the eardrums of every spectator. Folks covered their ears. One old man in a U.S.S. *Missouri* cap yelled, "Be done with it!"

After she belted the last line but before the recording finished, Lacey had disappeared.

Mother turned around to Dad and me. She shrugged then mouthed, "Hick rodeo."

Dad and I stepped down from the bleachers, pausing so that the Best Piece in Town girls could jiggle into a row. The tropical smell of coconut oil wafted around the unseasonably tan girls. Up close, they were all hair spray, cleavage, and fake eyelashes.

Before we got to the bottom step, Lacey appeared on the walkway. The hat was gone and her hair blew back from her face as she stomped toward Mother.

"I'm NEVER doing that again!" Lacey screamed. At our mother. At the bottom of the bleachers. In front of everyone.

A couple of the Best Piece in Town girls snickered, and it ticked me off. "What?" I flared up. "And you think your momma's proud?"

Dad squeezed my neck and turned me around. I scooted tightly against him, trying to block Lacey from the view of the crowd.

"NEVER!" Lacey's mascara dripped down her cheeks. "I'm never singing again."

One of the Best Piece in Town girls clapped.

Mother looked mad all over. Her French-manicured toes, peeking out from under the yellow strap, curled as if she were hanging on to the floor beneath her. "Lacey Diane Tillery," Mother hissed in a low voice, through her teeth. "Things go wrong in a performance. That's the music business. You want me to get you a straw so you can suck it up?"

Dad put his arm around Lacey and pulled her to his chest. "That's enough," he said. Dad held her to him and all but carried her out of the arena.

Mother clopped behind them in her fancy shoes and painted-on jeans.

I stood frozen at the bottom of the bleachers. My heart broke for Lacey. Not because she messed up, but because she had to be embarrassed and mad for not being true to herself.

When Mother handed her a microphone, Lacey should've grabbed a curling iron and stood her ground. If Lacey's disaster of a performance did anything good, it sure made me even more convinced that I had to drum. I was born to do it. Come hell or high water I was drumming at Texapalooza. I'd find out if I could hang with the best; then I'd set my course to be the best. Whatever and wherever it took me.

I held on to the railing a minute longer. The youth amateur bull riding was about to begin, and some boy in a black cowboy hat was easing onto a snorting, nasty white bull in the chute.

I watched it bang against the sides of the small chute, just itching for that gate to open. I knew the feeling of wanting to bust out. Let it fly with nothing to lose.

The announcer called out, "Ladies and gentlemen, we've got some local boys ready to ride."

I watched the bull chute. Bull riding was flat-out dangerous, and I'd known classmates who had more testosterone than sense to get their arms broken or teeth knocked out trying to beat eight seconds. But at the moment, I was pulling for the bull.

"Folks, you're in for a real treat," the announcer said. "Strapping on to White Lightning is a grandson of Colombian cowboy country. New to the area, hailing from the Granados Ranch in Paradise, Texas. Give it up for Gabriela Cordova Granados."

I ran down the walkway toward the chute end of the arena. *No way*, I thought. *It can't be him.*

The chute flew open and the bull sailed out in midair, spinning its tail end, then stomping its hind legs into the red dirt. Paradise held the rope with one hand, his other in the air. The bull threw him forward and back.

I grabbed the railing, jerking with every slinging move White Lightning had, willing Paradise a safe ride. Then the bull went into a death spin—turning like a crank.

The eight-second buzzer sounded just as Paradise began to slide off, his left wrist caught in the rope. But the buzzer meant nothing to White Lightning. He continued to swing his back end, violently twisting, as Paradise dangled by one arm at the end of the rope. The bull reared and stomped and dragged Paradise halfway across the arena, banging him around like a chew toy.

By the time the rope fell and freed his arm, Paradise lay still as death, facedown in the arena in a dusty fog of red dirt.

I grabbed my stomach. My jaws tingled and I thought I might puke. If Paradise hurt himself, he hurt the band.

A rodeo clown in patched-up overalls and a polka-dot blouse distracted White Lightning, luring him out of the arena. Two wranglers knelt down by Paradise.

The crowd, so loud and impressed with his ride, stood in prayerful silence. A few cowboys removed their hats.

Finally, Paradise rolled to his back. The wranglers helped him to his feet. Whistles and relieved clapping erupted as Paradise stood.

The idiot actually got up smiling, that little dimple teasingly creased. With his one good arm, he picked up his hat and waved it in big circles to the crowd.

I wanted to take the hat and smack him with it. The nut. He could've killed himself or broken an arm. Furthermore, if he did mess up his arm he probably messed up my chance at Texapalooza right along with it.

I made a beeline for the parking area behind the arena, forgetting about Lacey and my ride to the Tucker Barn. All I could think about was giving Paradise a piece of my mind.

6

THE PIECE-OF-MY-MIND GIRL

Behind the rodeo arena, rows of cars and trucks—some pulling horse trailers—turned the usually wildflower-covered field into a parking lot. I spotted Paradise's baby blue Bronco, the red-tipped petals of an Indian paintbrush barely escaping his front tire.

Paradise faced his Bronco. His one good hand pressed onto the hood. His legs were spread as one of the Best Piece in Town girls slapped the dust off the backside of his jeans.

She was the only thing keeping me from planting my boot square on his butt.

"Nice ride, Paradise." I stared at the rusty red rope burn on his right wrist, fighting the urge to kick him. "Unless you're in a band. Then it would be *stupid* ride, right?"

The girl looked back at me. Her black hair swirled in the wind like one of those shampoo models on TV. She was older, probably a student at the community college and probably thinking I was his little sister or something. She took one look at my minidress and boots and backed away from him as if to remove herself from a family squabble.

Paradise turned around. His hat was on. His shirt was off. His pants hung on his hips just below his chiseled waist. He leaned against the Bronco's grill stretching both arms across the hood.

"It's all good, Paisley." He made a fist and flexed his right wrist. "And it *was* a nice ride." He lay back on the hood, and hollered some ridiculous man howl. "OU-OOOOO!"

The Best Piece in Town girl twisted her long, silky hair into a rope and clutched it against her chest with both hands. "We'll talk later, Gabriela." She rolled her eyes at him then smiled as she passed me on her way back toward the rodeo arena.

Paradise seemed as unconcerned with her leaving as he was with the bull riding. His lackadaisical attitude toward life was just not going to fly with me.

"You need to understand a couple of things." I wanted to point at him, but the wind had really kicked up. I had to hold my dress down to keep it from flying above my head. "I risk a lot of family drama to be in the Waylon Slider Band. Playing at Texapalooza is it for me."

"That's a shame." Paradise rose up off the hood and hung the heel of his boot on the Bronco's bumper. "Can't you dream bigger than that?"

"This isn't about what I can do. It's about what you can do." I moved to the side of his Bronco. At least the bottom half of me would be out of the wind, and I wouldn't have to look at him anymore—the flirty little way his hair curled at the base of his neck, his washboard abs. I stood still for a moment, clearing my mind with the *wooooooosh* of the wind rushing through the tops of the pines edging the pasture. "You've agreed to be part of the band, so don't take any more stupid chances. Don't screw this up for the rest of us."

"Speaking of screwing up"—Paradise opened the passenger door and pulled out a neatly folded black T-shirt—"shouldn't you be at the Tucker Barn?" He pushed one arm through a sleeve and squeezed into the T-shirt, tight as bark on a tree.

"Are you just going to dress in front of me?"

"You don't have to watch." He tucked the front part of the shirt behind his belt buckle.

I spotted his murse in the backseat. A clean shirt and the accordion, Paradise was definitely headed to the Tucker Barn.

"Just you don't be late," I told him.

I gripped the bottom of my dress around my thighs and followed the tire tracks through the pasture parking lot, around the arena, almost to the entrance gate at the highway. I had ridden to the rodeo with Dad, but his truck was nowhere in sight. I scanned the lines of parked vehicles. Lacey's yellow Volkswagen Bug was gone too. And she definitely would not be inside with all those eyewitnesses to her meltdown.

Near the arched metal gate by the entrance, I climbed into the bed, then onto the cab of a jacked-up Dually. I had wasted too much time on Paradise. Now it was getting dark. The lights had come on around the arena. The wind and humidity in the spring air signaled a coming rain.

I sat down on top of the cab, trying to figure out what to do. Mother and Dad surely thought I was with Lacey. If I called home, they'd come and get me. But I'd miss the gig at the Tucker Barn. I tried texting Lacey on my cell. "Where r u?" No response. I texted Lacey three more times. No response. Unless I could find a ride, the Waylon Slider Band would be minus its drummer. Waylon would replace me. No doubt about it.

The headlights from a truck coming up the trail blinded me. I shielded my eyes with my forearm and waited for the truck and its thumping music to pass by. But the truck stopped. When I looked down, I saw the top of Paradise's baby blue Bronco.

I hopped off the cab and jumped off the side of the Dually. I jerked open the door to the Bronco and slid in.

"Don't say anything," I yelled over his music as I slammed the door. "I need a ride."

With the last of the sunshine gone and the spring storm clouds pressing in, Paradise drove onto the highway with me riding shotgun. He shifted into high gear then rested his arm on the back of the bench seat. His fingertips brushed my shoulder.

I straightened my dress, trying to cover my knees. There was something about Paradise that kept me in a constant state of agitation. It didn't help that he smelled sweet like boot leather and earthy musk, that everything about him—his perfect teeth, the jewel-toned emerald of his eyes, the little gold earrings—shimmered in the dark. It certainly didn't help that if I turned my head my cheek would press against his hand. As if my going to the Tucker Barn wasn't risky enough, I now had to contend with Paradise by the dashboard lights.

There were only two ways to get to the Tucker Barn. The back way, an old bootlegger road that crossed the Jessup County line, no one ever used. I turned his stereo down. "You know how to get there?"

"Yes, ma'am." Paradise moved his hand and turned the stereo back up.

Spanish music bounced from his speakers. But not like the music at Don Caliente's Taco Bar and Cantina. This was different.

I held my hand against one of the mounted speakers. A man's voice rapped Spanish lyrics. It was like pop or rock or both. Then I picked up, as identifiable as a steel guitar on a country song, the sound of an accordion driving the melody. And one other thing: a dull thumping I could feel through the speaker.

"Carlos Vives." Paradise smiled as he turned down the volume. "Hard not to like, right?"

"It's danceable. Kind of familiar." I kept my hand on the speaker and looked away from him, to the lightning flashes in the distance. "Like country rock."

"It is country rock. Colombian pop music with *vallenato*."

The headlights shined ahead spotlighting a huge oak tree to the right of the highway. A large sign with a red arrow came into view: TUCKER FAMILY VINEYARDS. Paradise shifted the Bronco into low, following the arrow and veering off the highway onto an old blacktop road.

Paradise slowed down and eased the Bronco over the rough, pot-holed road. I let go of the speaker. We were getting close to the Tucker Barn, deep in the woods where there are no streetlights, only the occasional glimpse of moonlight peeking through the treetops and the strobe-light flashes of lightning.

"What the heck is va-ye-whatever?"

"*Vallenato.* From Columbian cowboys. Think American country music. Story songs about love and loss and passion." He came to a stop at an old railroad crossing and looked down at my hands, my purity ring, and my fingers tapping away on my knees. "You do that a lot."

I stopped instantly, stupid nervous drumming, and moved to fidgeting with my hair. I tucked what I could behind my ears, pulling out a few little wispy pieces. I stared through the window at a distant radio tower with its red blinking lights.

"The barn's just ahead."

Paradise crossed the tracks. His *vallenato* played on.

I pressed my hand against the speaker again. I had to ask about the percussion. I couldn't stop myself. A drum of some kind I'd never heard before.

"What's that scraping sound? That beat?" I nodded my head as the speaker pulsed against my palm.

"The beat is a *caja*, a little drum." Paradise spread his fingers out above the steering wheel as if the drumhead were the same size as his hand. "The scraping sound is from a notched stick called a *guacharaca*." He whispered the Spanish word as if he just wanted to breathe it.

"A what?"

"A *gua-cha-ra-ca*." He wrestled with the steering wheel as he drove down the bumpy road. "Say it, *gua*—"

I tried my best, pursing my lips and blowing air to get the right sound. "Wa—wa . . ."

Paradise laughed and sped up. "Paisley, you look like a guppy fish."

I wanted to crawl onto the floorboard. Slink right out of the seat, out of his sight. *Guppy fish*. I let him reel me in when I should've been thinking about our gig. I should've been thinking about the drum setup. Would there be floor toms and hi-hat cymbals? I should've been thinking about that, or how in the heck I was going to get home. I shouldn't have been so caught up in Paradise or his music.

In a huff, I folded my arms at my waist. No more distractions.

We topped the hill about a mile away from the Tucker Barn. An orange glow, probably from a bonfire, hovered between the rolling hills. A twinge of nerves gripped me. I'd only been to the barn during the Tucker Winery's Annual Grape Stomp. I'd never come close to sneaking out to one of Levi's parties, and now I'd be there. Center stage. Bonfire, booze, and the band. I took a deep breath.

"You're good at drums, Paisley." Paradise seemed to get that he'd ticked me off. He put both hands on the wheel and served up some flattery. "My grandfather says that a good drummer is the heartbeat of *vallenato*." Paradise kept talking as if the way to this girl was through a percussion discussion. "The beat of the *caja* is the passion in the love story. The scraping of the *guacharaca* is the loss, the heartbreak. My grandfather says you can't play them until you've lived them."

"So," I started talking to him again. "Are you Colombian or something?"

"My mother is, and my grandfather." Paradise nodded at the murse that held his accordion in the backseat. "My grandfather is a *vallenato* king. A Colombian accordion king."

"Let me guess, that makes you the accordion prince?"

Paradise put one hand across his heart. "No, I'm more the accordion Prince Charming."

I could feel him catching glances at me as he drove, waiting for my reaction to his joke. But I didn't budge or say a word. Waiting and wondering would probably do the smart-ass some good.

Paradise tried sweetening my mood with drum talk again. "You play drums for your school band?"

"Yep." Tree branches clasped above the road making a cave-like tunnel through the wooded bottom. Paradise switched his lights to bright. I wondered about his school. "What about you? Can you play the accordion at school?"

Paradise turned his music down. "I used to. Anytime, any day."

"They kick you out for that?"

"*They* would be my grandfather and a tutor." Paradise sat up straighter when he mentioned his grandfather. "My parents traveled a lot. My dad didn't want me left in Colombia. My mother didn't want me left in Texas."

I shifted in my seat. "So you're homeschooled?" The thought of it terrified me. School was my solo venture out of the house and out of the Dripping Springs community.

"More like travel-schooled," Paradise started to explain but a loud rumble surrounded us.

I glanced at the side mirror. A car raced behind us, tailgating with the lights on bright. Paradise swerved to the side of the one-lane road, sending us into the brush and tall weeds that crowded the blacktop. A jeep full of kids zoomed past as Paradise stomped the brakes.

The sudden swerve slammed me into the side door. Before I could blink, Paradise reached across the seat.

"You all right, Paisley?" He gently squeezed the top of my leg, his fingertips pressing against the inside of my thigh.

"Yeah." I moved his hand off my leg and felt a sudden prickling of goose bumps. "I hope we ... I just hope we get out of the Tucker Barn alive."

Paradise eased back onto the road.

Maybe it was the moment, the talk of homeschooling, or my hand on his and the purity ring reflecting the moonlight, but I thought about my mother—at home, filling my and Lacey's Easter baskets with little-girl trinkets. Lacey would have hair ribbons; I'd have barrettes. We'd both have some new lip gloss and summer pajamas. She'd give Lacey a collection of samples from the gift-with-purchase promos run by the makeup counters at the mall. And even though it pained her, she'd place in my basket new drumsticks for me to use at school. She couldn't possibly imagine that I was out roaming backcountry roads with a boy, an older boy at that, on my way to drum for the Waylon Slider Band's first gig.

"You sure you're all right?"

I nodded.

We sped through an *S* curve, coming out of the woods into wide-open river bottom. Cars and trucks parked along the road and in the pasture. On a rise about two hundred yards inside a barbed-wire fence, the Tucker Barn—with its roof painted like the Texas flag and outlined in Christmas-tree lights—twinkled like Barbie's Redneck Playhouse.

I forgot all about Mother and steadied myself for a party in the pasture.

7

PASTURE PARTY
BREAKDOWN

The burning end of cigarettes pulsed like the orange flash of fire-flies among the cars lined along the fence row. In the low part of the pasture, jacked-up mud trucks circled a raging bonfire—flames firing at least twenty feet into the black night. And one tip end of Moon Lake glowed in the distance. Kids from all over the tri-county area showed up. From the blessed to the broke. Paradise stopped at the cattle guard and handed one of Levi's brothers ten bucks. Between the band and the kegs, the Tucker boys turned a profit.

Paradise followed the dirt road up the hill and around the barn, parking on the back side. I opened the door to the Bronco. The minute I put one boot down on Tucker soil, lightning struck, splitting the night sky in two with its jagged white bolt.

Paradise jumped. His hat slipped off, and the wind sent it bouncing like tumbleweed between the parked cars and trucks. I chased it down and handed the dusty Stetson back to him.

I loved the crash of lightning, the cannonball rolling of thunder—even the brushing of a soft rain or a crackling hailstorm. I stood, lost in the rumble, gazing at the white Texas moon slowly disappearing behind the churning gray-black storm clouds.

"God's a drummer." I smiled at Paradise.

He ran his fingers through his black hair and pushed his hat firmly down on his head. "Maybe so." He swung his murse over his shoulder. "But the angels play accordion."

I had to laugh but I didn't want him to see it. He'd certainly be hard to handle if he thought he could get to me. I shook my head and looked down at my boots, the ground, anywhere but his face. But he caught my grin anyway and took my face in his hand. The tips of his fingers rested on my cheek. "You should laugh more, Paisley." He slowly stroked his thumb along my bottom lip. "This crooked little smile of yours is . . ."

I grabbed his wrist and felt his braided leather bracelet and the racing of his pulse. "Keep your hands on your accordion." As the spring storm blew in around us, I stood in the prickling rain certain of nothing but the need to draw a line in the sand where he was concerned. Like Colonel William B. Travis at the Alamo. Make a clear boundary that Paradise was not to cross. I let loose of his wrist and started toward the front of the barn. "We've got a show to put on."

Whatever just happened confused me. The more I thought about it, the faster I walked. But he managed to keep the same pace, ambling beside me with his long-legged stride. He wasn't going anywhere. I tried to train my thoughts on our performance and Texapalooza. One step at a time; keep my eyes on the prize. But Paradise wasn't going anywhere. And Colonel Travis lost.

Guys and girls huddled in groups all across the pasture, most in the shadows of the bonfire. We slipped between two trucks. The doors were open; the tailgates were down. A large galvanized bucket sat on one truck's tailgate with a tower of Dixie cups next to it.

One of Lacey's classmates stood by the truck. "Hey, Tillery!" The older boys always called me by my last name. He dipped a cup in the bucket and handed it to me as I walked by. "Take this to your sister."

I kept walking until I was out of his sight and nearly to the front of the barn. I had no clue where Lacey was, and even if I did, I wouldn't be loading her up with bucket booze.

Paradise started laughing. "Purple Jesus," he said. "That stuff'll make you think you can walk on water."

I sniffed it. "Smells like grape Kool-Aid."

"Plus a whole lot more. It's trash-can punch, Paisley. A bunch of different alcohols mixed together with grape Kool-Aid. And if you're not going to drink it, I will."

Thunder rolled over the pasture like a crashing boulder. I turned the cup upside down and poured it out.

"Nice," Paradise said. He stomped toward the barn.

I followed behind him. "Not everyone comes out here to get drunk."

He threw his head back and laughed.

"Wait a minute." I grabbed his arm. His skin was moist from the wet night air. "That's not why we're here."

The rain began to come down harder.

The kids in the pasture made a sudden push for the barn. The roof's overhang created two long porches on each side, wide and deep enough to park a travel trailer. Plenty of room for everyone to take shelter. I wanted to hurry and get there too. Not so much to get out of the rain, but more to get under the metal roof and let the rain drum over me. I was ready to play. I'd been thinking about it all day long, craving the way the pulse rolls out of me and bounces off the drums. I played because that rhythm, that sound, had to get out. A pounding ache pummeled inside me. Everything made more sense to me from behind the drums.

"PAISLEY!"

Waylon and Levi stood just under the porch. Levi had his overalls tucked in his rubber boots like he was hoping for a chance to get in the mud. Right above Levi's head, a pistol-shaped wooden sign was nailed to a support post: WE DON'T CALL 911. Running the length of the barn's side, a series of three double doors was flung wide-open. Inside the barn, a neon Shiner Bock sign highlighted the party crowd. All my life, I'd heard about generations of Tucker kids and their parties. Now I was here. I could smell the perfume mixed with cigarette smoke, feel the thumping bass from the band inside—an energy I could grasp. And the steady rain on the barn's tin roof. Almost as intoxicating as the cowboy who drove me here.

"Dang, Paisley!" Levi leaned against the post and laughed as Paradise and I walked together. Levi held up a Mason jar half full of a crystal-clear liquid like he was making a toast, his eyes darting from Paradise to me. "When you cut out from under your momma, you make a clean break."

"It's not what you think." I stepped away from Paradise.

Waylon blurted, "Your sister got here an hour ago."

"Yeah, well." I kept my eyes fixed on the pack of kids crowded inside the bar-like barn. "She left the rodeo in a hurry." I was sure they had already heard about Lacey butchering the national anthem at the rodeo and would just move on off that topic. But no.

"You gonna have to drive her home, Paisley." Levi picked at a splinter in the wooden post. "She's been doing Jell-O shots since she got here."

I knew then that I had to find her. I started past Levi and he stopped me.

"Everybody understands. We're watching her," he assured me. "I ain't takin' my eyes off her other than to play this one set."

"Not really anything new with Lacey," Waylon added as he fiddled with a brown skull cap that covered his wiry hair and made him look older. He kept taking it off and on like he wasn't sure if it was what he really wanted to wear. Without a guitar strapped around him, Waylon had no self-confidence.

"Just keep it on." I made the decision for him.

"When does the band break?" Paradise asked.

"In about five minutes," Waylon said.

"That's enough time to get loose." Paradise smiled at Levi and reached out for the Mason jar.

"Oh, heck no!" I couldn't believe he was serious. The last thing we needed was a drunk, lead-singing accordion player.

Waylon pointed his finger at Paradise. "If you want to drink, you can do it *after* we play."

Paradise ignored both of us and took a sip. Immediately, his face twisted like a soaked mop being wrung out. He grabbed Levi's shoulder and kicked the heel of his boot against the concrete.

"This ain't vodka." Levi took his jar back.

The *ping* of a drummer's rim shot rang out from inside the barn to the breezeway porch where we stood.

"Nobody drinks before we play!" Waylon commanded.

Paradise started laughing, lost his hat, and fell face-first into Levi's chest.

"How can you drink that stuff?" he mumbled as he straightened back up.

"An acquired taste." Levi sipped from the jar, showing his teeth as he swallowed.

"Forget it." Waylon threw his hands up. "We're not playing."

With that, the reality of playing in my first gig, my chance at drumming at Texapalooza crashed. My opportunity to perform was as much in Waylon's control as a kite is at the mercy of the wind.

But I held on. I hadn't showed up here and risked being home-schooled for nothing.

"No, Waylon, wait." I stared hard at Levi. He gave Paradise his hat back. "They're done drinking."

I knew Waylon's obsessive-compulsive tendencies and under-stood that too often they kept him from stepping out. If he thought for a minute the Waylon Slider Band would stink it up, Waylon would pull the plug. Waylon needed to believe that we'd throw down a solid show, and I had enough faith in that to carry all of us.

"We can do this, Waylon."

He clasped his hands on top of his head, pushing his skull cap down like he was trying to keep whatever was going on in that per-fectionist mind of his under control.

"You know we're good enough."

Levi patted Waylon on the back. "I spit ninety proof, brother. You know that. I ain't ever been too drunk to play."

"You're not the problem." Then Waylon cut his eyes at Paradise.

"I can become a lot bigger problem for you." Paradise threw his shoulders back and the muscles in his neck hardened. He seemed to have a hot button when it came to Waylon's laying out band rules. The last thing we needed was someone fighting Waylon for control of his own band.

I stepped in between them. "They're done drinking. That's all that matters, right?"

"Just be there when the first band finishes." Waylon stomped off. "I'm going to find Cal."

Paradise gripped the strap of his murse as if he wasn't sure what he wanted to do with that accordion. He looked ticked off like he wasn't accustomed to having boundaries placed on his behavior. Keeping his ego in check wasn't going to be easy. I might have to struggle with my mother when it came to drumming. But Paradise, it seemed, had a bigger problem: himself.

I stood boot tip to boot tip with him and looked up. "I'm taking this opportunity to remind you one more time." The brim of his hat shaded the light and I could feel his breath on my face. "This isn't about you. It's about the band. If you want to play, be an accordion king or whatever, then just be respectful of the rest of us." I took a deep breath. "Please."

I waited for him to say something—some smart-aleck comeback, some flirty suggestion. But I got nothing. He just gazed out across the field at the sheets of pouring rain, then walked off.

I followed him inside the barn, not sure what he was about to do. Hoping I hadn't pushed him too far. It was dark and loud and crowded, and I squeezed my way between folks, trying not to lose Paradise. A dance-floor area had been outlined with hay bales, but he didn't head that direction. Instead, I found him by a flatbed trailer that had been turned into a stage. I found him by the band.

Paradise had his arms folded at his waist and his feet a little more than shoulder width apart. He studied the lead singer as the dude sweated and screamed his way through what I hoped was their final song.

I walked up and tugged on his arm. "So, you thinking about quitting us and joining the shirtless band?" All the guys, except for their bassist, had their shirts off.

Paradise gestured toward the drummer—a skinny dude with tribal tats inked across his shoulders. "You're better than that."

I watched the drummer. "He's all wrist." I started to stretch out my arms. Volume comes from power. Power starts in the core. I thought about the great drummers I'd watched. The sticks are just an extension of the arms. Using only the wrist is like driving a Mustang in first gear. "He may be tatted up like Travis Barker, but he should spend more time watching him."

Paradise fixed his eyes back on the lead singer who, in an attempt to work the crowd, was stomping from one side of the trailer to the other.

From what little I'd seen, Paradise had his own style—a sexy way of drawing up to a microphone. This lead singer seemed to be trying to imitate the front man from his favorite rock band. "You're better than that," I told Paradise.

Paradise shrugged. "Maybe. But playing accordion and having people respect what I play is all I really care about."

The lead singer finished screaming and slumped to his knees as his drummer rolled to a stop.

Levi and Waylon snuck up behind us. Cal was with them, holding his Gibson by the neck.

"Is this your band?" the lead singer asked Levi as he hopped off the trailer.

"Yeah, man," Levi answered. "Actually we're the Waylon Slider Band. This is Waylon."

If the dude was from this area and knew his music, he'd know the Slider name. Waylon wiped his hand on his jeans and stuck it out to shake with him.

But it seemed Tucker was the only name he cared about. "Don't screw up our stuff, Levi."

The drummer stepped off the trailer and held up his sticks. "Who gets the keys to the kingdom?"

I raised my hand like a third grader.

He handed me the sticks. "Don't tighten any of the heads. Don't adjust anything. You can lower the throne but that's it."

Paradise jumped onto the trailer and headed for an Oriental rug laid out in the center. Waylon, Levi, and Cal followed and made a beeline for their spots. I stepped behind the drums and looked out into the crowded barn. I'd played in front of crowds before at band concerts and football games. I'd even had solos on the snare. But this was my chance to see what I could do outside of a school-controlled performance and obligatory applause.

I turned the knob on the stool and lowered it.

This was my moment of truth. A real beginning. A line in the sand with my own dream.

8

BLINDED BY THE LIGHT

From my seat behind the drums, the mass of kids in the dark barn reminded me of the time when the lights went out during a basketball game at the school gym: pitch-black except for the neon glow of exit signs and the faceless outlines of friends. Although a bit of porch light hovered around each of the side doors, very little drifted in.

I scooted the stool forward, centering it on the snare, and repositioned the foot pedals. I ran my hands across each drumhead. The basic right-handed setup, so I was good to go—even if the trailer stage was darker than what I'd prefer.

Plunk-plunks ricocheted as Waylon and Cal thumbed their guitar strings in tune.

"Now, y'all don't get going without me." Levi rested the bass guitar on a stand, jumped off the trailer, muscled his way between the drunk and disorderly, and headed for the back of the barn.

Paradise stood in front of the drums with his hands on his hips. He turned to me and pointed to the line of tractors and heavy equipment stored at the back of the barn. Levi had climbed into the cab of an International Harvester combine.

Paradise pushed his hat low on his forehead. "Close your eyes, Paisley."

In that instant, the combine's roof lights switched on—putting a spotlight right on the band, right on us.

A loud moan broke through the barn as the tractor's high beams shattered the comfortable darkness. I kept my head down until my eyes adjusted. When I finally looked back up, Levi had lowered the beams to dim. A softer light hung just above the heads of the crowd and broadened right as it reached us. It was the perfect spotlight, and Levi looked proud of himself.

He hopped back onto the trailer, still wearing his rubber boots, with a smile as wide as a barn door. "Can't nobody say Tuckers ain't re-sourceful."

Now that I had some light, I realized the ride cymbal was too high for me to hit the center crown. I wouldn't be able to get a full-enough sound for the choruses if I didn't drop it. I checked each side of the stage. No sign of the previous band.

Paradise was strapped into his accordion and standing a few steps in front of the drums.

"Over here." I pointed just above the ride cymbal.

He took a couple of back steps and blocked the light.

I glanced around one more time for the other band members or drummer. Then I lowered the ride.

Paradise started laughing. "Bad girl, Paisley. Isn't there some kind of Jesus code or Jesus bracelet about honesty or doing the right thing?"

"Shut up." I sat back down on the stool and laid the sticks on the snare. "If you want to know what Jesus says, go to church. I don't think bracelet reminders would help you much."

"Then why do you wear that ring?"

God, I hated it when he brought up my ring! Suddenly, I felt like I was in the nude trying to have a conversation with him. Like I wanted to openly discuss abstinence with His Royal Hotness on a stage before our first gig. I tried to ignore him.

Paradise took a sideways glance at Levi who hadn't picked up the bass yet. Waylon and Cal were still tuning. "Seriously, Paisley," he started picking at me again. "Aren't you under some evangelical witness obligation to teach me about these things? I mean, I need some Jesus guidance."

"Oh my gosh." I hopped to my feet, mostly out of frustration, but I wanted to make sure he heard me loud and clear. He was just a little too interested in my purity ring. I yelled at him, "I do not want to talk about having sex with you!"

My voice rang out through the barn as I stood in the tractor spotlight. I heard myself in the echo—*having sex with you, sex with you . . .*

I dropped the drumsticks.

A few whistles and some clapping rose from the crowd onto the stage.

"Hot microphone, sweetheart." Paradise laughed.

I caught sight of Waylon out of the corner of my eye—his mouth gaped open. Even Cal stared at me.

"I didn't mean that the way it came out." I held my hand up to show Waylon, Levi, and Cal what I was talking about. "He asked about my ring. I was trying to explain that. Abstinence. Really!"

Suddenly, nothing felt right. My first instinct was to run off the stage and throw a chair.

Waylon stepped in front of the drums. "Paisley." His shoulders were back; his guitar strap with SLIDER tooled into the leather hung across his chest. He was battle ready. "Keep your personal stuff personal. We need you to do a job. Just do it. Don't get caught up with what the audience thinks. They think the band is done. Most of them are drunk anyway. Tonight is about us putting what we do out there and making sure our sound is solid."

There was no point in my arguing my case anymore. Mother's lectures to Lacey played over in my head. *Stuff goes wrong in a performance. That's just the business.* And Waylon was right about the crowd. They weren't really paying us much attention at all. I sat down in front of the snare and picked up the sticks. Nylon tips. I preferred wood. I tapped them together; the pitch matched. If my sound wasn't even, I couldn't blame the sticks. I slipped my right foot onto the bass drum pedal. I had this. I was good to go.

A sound like a howling wind raced around the barn. Paradise was warming up. Against his black T-shirt, the red accordion shined in the light. He held it between his muscular arms, pushing and pulling and sailing his fingers across the button keys.

"Let's do this," Waylon said. He gathered everyone in front of the drums. "We play like we practice. Nothing fancy. Solid. Cal, you open with 'Sweet Child O'Mine.' Then we move to our songs." Waylon kept on, "We don't have to be great, just good." And he kept on, "This is just like the hangar."

Sometimes I thought Waylon's experience in performing got in the way of his actual performing. He analyzed everything down, shredding each minute detail. Being a Slider, he probably had more to lose from a bad performance than any of us, so I always tried to respect his lectures.

But Paradise was done with Waylon.

Paradise turned his back and snaked up to the center microphone. "Everybody put your hands in the air!" His voice boomed throughout the barn. Unlike Waylon, Paradise was all into the crowd.

I wasn't sure what he was up to, but I gripped a stick in each hand. Cal and Levi scrambled to their places. Waylon's face went scarlet. He looked as if he wanted more than anything to slap a five star on Paradise's back and shove him face-first off the trailer.

Paradise started clapping his hands above his head until what sounded like a good many in the crowd joined in. "Give me a beat!"

OK, that was *my* job, and this was not at all what we had practiced. I had no idea what he'd pull next.

I watched Waylon with his guitar slung loosely across his body and his hands on his hips. I honestly thought he might self-combust. Just burst into a flame right there on the flatbed-trailer stage in the Tucker Barn.

Then Paradise did the unbelievable. He started singing. A cappela. No intro from Cal, no hint of anything we'd practiced. No nothing other than the steady, sloppy clapping of a bunch of drunk teenagers. He began flapping his arms in an upward motion, which was apparently our cue to start playing.

Cal caught up with him. Levi looked back at me, trying to lock in a beat for his bass. I went for it—hitting the bass drum and the snare and the hi-hats in regular time. I sounded like a lazy horse clopping along a brick street, but it was all I could do. So much for rocking out. No syncopations. No fancy fills. I was drumming myself to sleep.

Paradise sang his face off. I'll give him that much. The crowd, seduced by his slow grooving cover of "Sweet Child O'Mine," dipped and swayed. But he left no room for the rest of us. Even Cal, who could harmonize with bawling cattle, kept silent. This show belonged to Paradise. The Waylon Slider Band was just background.

Paradise rolled right out of Guns N' Roses and straight into one of Waylon's songs. He owned it like he'd written it himself. Had the words memorized, sang like the words meant something to him personally, and never once looked back. He never cocked his head to Cal or Waylon to transition. He just steamrolled his way through, confident that we would back him up. And when he keyed up his accordion, he became a one-man show. It didn't matter to me how good he was. The whole thing sucked.

It was probably close to eleven thirty, and I yawned through my own boring beat. Levi shook his head at Waylon while Paradise blew into a fiery squeezebox solo. Really impressive. Even the first band crowded the side of the trailer and watched him in amazement.

Whoopee.

The crowd, drunk or not, clapped louder as he played. Stomped their boots. A hard, steady pounding that rocked the barn. He had his own freaking mosh pit. Cal tried to weave his way into the spotlight, but every time he got near a corner of that fancy rug, Paradise just squeezed the accordion faster and harder. Like one of those ridiculous Chia pets that sprouts when drenched with water, Paradise seemed to grow bigger as the crowd poured on the encouragement.

Finally, Waylon held up his index finger. One more song and we were all done.

The Waylon Slider Band played it out. I finished it off with a soft flam, a rim shot, and a punch to the bass drum. Like the end of a bad joke. *Ba-da-bing.*

Waylon took his guitar and jumped off the stage. Cal unplugged his Gibson from the amp, took a rubber band from his wrist, and pulled his hair back.

Paradise turned around as if he'd suddenly remembered he forgot something important and now it was nowhere to be found. "What's the deal?" He put his hands on his hips. "That was only a few songs. We're not done."

"You may not be." I hopped off the trailer; my boots slapped the concrete. "But the rest of us are."

Paradise peeled the accordion off his chest. "What? You're all quitting?"

I handed the sticks to the drummer from the first band.

"You did the right thing," the drummer said to me, then looked up at Paradise. "Quit shit, man. She stayed in the pocket for you. I would've left your arrogant ass up there with no backbeat."

I forced my way through the crowd. It was getting late. I just wanted to find Lacey and go home.

Pat Green's "Carry On" ripped through the barn. Levi must've loaded up the sound system, looking to get loose and lost in his playlist of Texas country.

Fine with me. Carry on was just what I intended to do. I was done with Paradise.

I stopped and asked a couple of kids I knew were in my sister's senior English class, "Have you seen Lacey?"

They shook their heads and went right back to singing along with Levi's soundtrack.

I stood on one of the hay bales marking off the dance floor. Thought maybe I'd find her dancing. She was nowhere in the line of couples rounding.

As I stepped down from the hay bale, the fluorescent lights flickered on without warning and lit up the entire barn. Kids began to flood out through each of the side doors.

"Paisley!" Levi yelled as he, Waylon, and Cal ran toward me. "Get on home. Sheriff's deputies are down at the gate handing out MIPs."

I stared up at the roof of the barn. Fought back mad tears, scared tears. Minor in Possession. I was a pasture length away from getting slapped with a ticket for being a minor with alcohol. The fact that I hadn't been drinking wasn't going to get in the way of a fund-raising opportunity for the sheriff. I was in the vicinity. Close enough.

Maybe this was God's way of saying, *Hey, Paisley. Listen to your mother. Drumming's not for you. You'll just get in with the wrong crowd and get in trouble.*

How would I ever explain an MIP to my mother? How would I explain the band? Then I remembered Lacey.

"I can't leave without my sister."

Waylon jumped square in my face. "Get over it, Paisley. Get out," he yelled, pointing toward the barn doors. "I've gotta have you on drums."

Cal put his hand on Waylon's shoulder. Waylon shrugged it off and stomped away, disappearing into the scrambling kids.

"I'm sorry, Paisley." Levi looked down at his rubber boots. "Look, they'll Breathalyze you, and you ain't been drinkin'. Maybe your momma'll cut you some slack."

"Her mother won't have to." Paradise brushed against my back.

"You've got that bootlegger road that cuts across the Jessup County line and hits the highway. Take the Bronco."

He handed his keys to Levi, but Levi kept his hands behind the bib of his overalls. He'd had enough of Paradise too.

"Thanks but no thanks." I had enough of choices being made for me at home. "Not your decision." I wasn't about to stand there and let a bunch of guys call the shots either. But the bootlegger road was a way out. "Levi, Lacey's car is here. I can find her and drive us through."

Levi shook his head. "That little Bug ain't gonna make it over the trail, especially after this rain."

The crowd inside the barn thinned. I looked past Levi. Cal was long gone, but Waylon was coming back. And he was coming back with my sister.

"Lacey!" My heart pounded. Shook my whole chest.

Barely able to sling one foot in front of the other, Lacey hung like a discarded rag doll against Waylon. Her blond curls exhausted into yarn-like mats. Her ruffled shirt buttoned awkwardly in only two places. All the rumors I'd heard about her, about my own sister, stared me in the face. Rumors are one thing. I'd blown them off because mostly they came from girls at school who looked down on us, on any rural kid who claimed a post office box instead of a street address. But there was no shirking off what I could reach out and touch.

"I found her on the bench outside." Waylon shifted his eyes from Levi, got defensive. "She was just like this, I swear. I guess whoever she was with figured that she couldn't run."

I heard Levi mutter something that sounded an awful lot like "I'll kill 'em."

I brushed the matted hair away from Lacey's face. A black

mascara smudge darkened her cheekbone and temple. I wiped and wiped as much away as I could with my fingers. But I couldn't wipe away the pain that someone had used her and tossed her like trash. I wanted to make her right.

No way could I let our folks see her like that.

"Paisley, take the Bronco." Paradise put his hand on my shoulder. The muscles in his neck quivered. "I want to help."

9

ON THE RUN

My heart set its beat to the warning light cadence from the police cars barricading the pasture gate. Blue—red. Blue—red. Blue—red. I slipped around the back of the barn. Following Paradise and Levi. Staring at the ground. The rain-soaked night wrapped around me like a cold, soggy towel.

It occurred to me to quit.

Just.

Quit.

It wasn't like I could name any rural girls who'd ever gone off and made a name for themselves drumming. I could do other things. Things I wouldn't have to hide. Things that maybe even made more sense. Practical things with predictable outcomes.

Truck doors slammed all across the pasture as our footsteps pounded the ground in a half-time shuffle. I could so play that groove; just hit the snare on the third beat.

A sharp chill cut through me, but it was no night wind. I could quit the drums, but rhythm would haunt me forever.

I ran to catch up to Levi and Paradise. Drumming was in my core, and I knew that I couldn't let it go. No matter what happened on the other side of the two-rut road leading into the pines.

Levi had hoisted Lacey over his shoulder, carried her from the barn. He laid her in the backseat of the Bronco. He knelt over her for a long time, smoothing her hair, until finally slamming the door shut.

Paradise opened the driver's-side door. "I'll be at the bottom of the hill just down from your uncle's place. Where that wooden bridge is."

Lacey's key chain, the one with the giant silver heart, dangled from his middle finger.

I scooted behind the wheel. "I owe you for this."

Regardless of how selfish I thought he was onstage, Paradise was willing to drive Lacey's car past the sheriff and take an MIP for me. And I was desperate enough to let him.

Lacey moaned from the backseat; then she giggled some. As if it wasn't bad enough that her shirt was buttoned wrong, the top button on her jeans was undone. Nothing about this night was right. One big cluster bomb.

I tried to put it all out of my head—the band was screwed, my sister was screwed. If I couldn't make the cut through the woods, I'd be screwed. I hunted around for the ignition, but I just couldn't find it, and my legs weren't nearly long enough to reach the pedals, and I thought in that moment that I would scream. Scream my lungs out. I slammed both hands on the steering wheel.

"Easy now." Paradise pitched his hat into the passenger seat and took the keys from me. He leaned in, reaching toward the floor-board, jerked on a handle, and popped the seat forward. "Put your foot on the brake and push the clutch in."

Brake. Clutch. I tried to think of it like my drums—just working the hi-hats with one foot and the bass pedal with the other.

Paradise stuffed the key in the ignition and cranked the engine. Then he grabbed the doorframe with one hand and pushed himself out. "Don't take whatever's going on in that blond head of yours out on my ride."

"Levi!" someone hollered from the barn. "Two sheriff's deputies are headed this way."

Levi stared through the window at Lacey sprawled in the backseat. He let down the straps to his overalls, slipping them from his sturdy shoulders. Levi took off his shirt, opened the side door, and covered her.

Paradise held open the door as if he was having second thoughts, like maybe driving Lacey's car out and taking an MIP wasn't such a smart move on his part. "Stay in the ruts and out of the brush," he said. "Try not to bounce around too much."

He locked his eyes with mine, pursed his lips, and blew a soft whistle. "My accordion's in the back."

"Get on out, Paisley." Levi stood behind Paradise. "Keep your lights off as long as the moonlight holds out. And don't stop in that thicket for nobody or nothin'."

I let up on the clutch and leaned on the gas. I stayed in low gear as I followed the old bootleg road into the woods. *Nobody, nothing. Jason, Freddy, Michael Myers. Maybe clowns. I hate clowns.*

I pushed on. Rolling over the deep ruts was a little like crawling across gravel on my hands and knees. And it hurt like that too. It hurt because this shouldn't be how chasing a dream goes down for me or Lacey or anybody else. If I didn't have to hide my drumming or the band, I wouldn't be in this mess. Lacey might even be sober.

The trees crowded against the Bronco. The moonlight disappeared. I'd driven downhill, deep into the wooded bottom, into a cave-like darkness so black that I couldn't see my hand in front of my face. The night's rain pooled in the bottom, turning it into a soaked swamp. Water sloshed against the tires. I had to hit the lights or lose the trail.

I grabbed for the headlight switch but got the turn indicator. Blinking left. Blinking right. I slowed to a creep as I hunted for the lights.

With no warning, just a jarring thud, the right front tire slammed into a hole. My neck snapped forward as I hit the brake. No clutch. The Bronco coughed and choked to a dead silence in the deep woods. Levi's warning not to stop snuck up on me. I pushed my back hard against the seat, sinking lower.

Lacey started singing, "Oh-o, say can you see-eeee . . ."

"Shut up, Lacey." I pushed in the clutch, turned the ignition key, pressed the accelerator. The engine roared.

"By-y the dawn's early li-ight."

With one foot on the brake and one on the clutch, I hit the blinkers again. Still no lights.

Lacey hummed for a few seconds; then she grunted as if she was trying to get up.

No way would I be able to drive us out and corral her at the same time.

"Shut up, Lacey. Please. Just lay down."

I tried clearing my mind, focused on finding the freakin' lights. But she just wouldn't stop moaning and grunting.

I whipped around.

Lacey was flat on her back across the seat and silent. Not a movement. Not a word. But the grumbling, a deep huffing grunt, continued all around the Bronco.

I slammed the lock down on my side, reached across, locked the passenger door.

Twigs snapped in the darkness. A sliver of moonlight sliced through the trees. The thicket shook. Whatever was coming was heavy footed. Not alone.

Sweat dampened my neck. A cold bead snaked down my spine.

I revved the engine and slapped at the dash. I found a knob, twisting and turning it and finally pulling it out.

The headlight beams burst into the thicket. I shrieked. Four. No. Six feral hogs—the size of stocky bulls—darted in the brightness and charged the Bronco.

"I gotta go pee," Lacey mumbled.

WAP. WAP. Lacey slapped at the door. If she got ahold of that handle, got out, the hogs would mangle her.

"NO! God, Lacey please." Keeping my foot on the brake, I shifted into neutral and let off the clutch. I reached over the seat and grabbed her arm. "If you never listen to me again, just lay back down."

Lacey looked at me like she didn't know who I was. Then she fell back. Passed out.

When I turned around, I could see the trail ahead blocked by a hulking black hog. A male one with tusks. Pissed off. Its nostrils flaring with every angry huff.

I pushed in the clutch, wrestled the stick shift into low gear, goosed the accelerator. Nothing budged. Not the Bronco's right front tire. Not the wild hog.

"C'mon." I tried reverse. Maybe back out of the hole. The tire barely budged. The other front tire squealed as it spun deeper into the mud.

"Crap." I knew what I had to do. Gun it and get out of the hole. But I didn't know if the hog would move. Hitting it would be like hitting a wall head-on.

I couldn't honk. If I did, the sheriff's deputies would know we'd hightailed out the back way. Lacey and I would be in trouble twice as deep for running.

I had no choice.

I gutted it up, squeezed the steering wheel with both hands, floored the accelerator. The front end heaved as the Bronco shot out of the hole, straight toward the hog. I hung on, but I could feel the back tires losing traction on the wet, red clay trail. The hog bolted into the brush as the Bronco slid into a sideways drift. Like we'd hit ice. I turned the steering wheel into the slide, trying to counter the drift, trying to keep out of the trees. The tires spun. Clods of mud hailed down on us. Pummeling the roof. I fought the slide with everything I had. Staying off the brake. Holding the steering wheel steady. Wrecking was not an option.

I held my breath and rode the drift until I felt the back end swing into line. I steered the Bronco into an opening flanked by two old oaks, their gnarled branches forming an archway.

The trail had disappeared beneath the rutting and the hoof stamping of the wild hogs. I pushed in the clutch, eased on the brake, and collapsed onto the steering wheel. My forehead damp from sweat. My shoulders ached from fighting with the steering wheel. But I had to get out of the thicket.

The Jessup County line couldn't be that much farther ahead. If I was right, the highway would be just a rock's throw from the woods' edge. If I was wrong, I'd be tunneling deeper into the piney woods. Dad would have the sheriff and his dogs searching by church time Easter Sunday. I'd be legendary, but for all the wrong reasons.

I shut off the headlights. Just sat there in the black night, clutching the steering wheel, my head resting on my hands. The hogs had scattered. Lacey was out. Not even a coyote howling. It was just me and a trembling fear I couldn't shake.

I sat upright and looked at my hands. My worst fear wasn't of wild hogs, psycho movie murderers, or MIPs. It wasn't even the getting caught. All that seemed to disappear into the woods with the hogs. There was only one thing. The real fear. The worst fear.

I tilted the rearview mirror and stared at my sister's reflection.

There was nothing I feared in the woods that scared me more than not being able to drum in the band—to make something of myself—and I'd hang on to drumming and the band with my teeth if I had to.

I wasn't going to stay stuck in the woods. Nothing could keep me from making it.

I turned the lights back on and stepped out of the Bronco.

The trees looked different in the night with their bark bright-lighted to an ash gray. I searched around, three-sixty, until I was certain the way to the highway was between the arching oaks. I hopped back into the Bronco and set out.

About a hundred yards farther into the thicket, the trees began to thin, the canopy opened up to a broad star-filled sky. The storm front had pushed through. The clear night behind it breathed a soft blue moonlight onto the pasture ahead. I sucked in a deep breath. The curving highway, slick from the rain and shining like black glass, waited at the end of the trail like a shiny-shoed escort extending the bend of his arm.

I pulled onto the road and exhaled. I could make it now. Dodged a bullet. The dream was still alive.

10

HANGING ON AND HANGING IN

I steered with one hand, reached over the seat, and patted her leg.

"Lacey, wake up."

She grumbled and began to stir, wrapping Levi's shirt around her shoulders.

"Get up and get yourself together. We're almost home." I took a right off the highway onto the blacktop county road. "I'm switching cars at the bridge by L. V.'s."

At the bottom of the hill, just before L. V.'s house, I spotted Lacey's yellow Volkswagen. Paradise leaned against the side; Cal sat on the edge of the roadside out from under the trees. He had a piece of paper pressed on his leg and looked like he was trying to write by the moonlight.

I drove onto the old wooden bridge and stopped. The boards creaked, but the tall cypress would camouflage the Bronco in case L. V. took a late-night smoke and stroll around his house.

Lacey sat up, rubbing her face. "I'm gonna . . . gonna bust if I don't pee." Lacey flung open the door. She put one pink boot on the bridge and fell to her knees.

I killed the engine and got out. Paradise helped her to her feet. She still wasn't completely right.

"Lacey, we're on the bridge. You're drunk. You'll have to wait till we get home."

She shook her arms loose from Paradise. "I ain't drunk and I'm going to pee."

Arguing with her would take too long, so I grabbed her shoulders and nudged her toward a stand of big trees. "Go. Just go." I'd made it through the woods and I wasn't about to let Lacey cut loose with some L. V.–alerting, drunken rant. I'd come too far to let my plans get messed up over Lacey's need to piss.

Paradise and I stayed out of view of Lacey on one side of the Bronco.

Cal still sat by the road. His long blond hair whipping around him in the night wind. "Looks like you got Cal out too," I said.

"For a skinny guy"—Paradise rubbed his beefy forearm—"that boy's a beast on guitar."

The pink corner of a piece of paper stuck out the pocket of Paradise's jeans.

"Is that your MIP?"

"Yeah. I'll do some community service for a few weeks. It's not that bad."

"Are your parents going to freak?"

He shook his head and laughed, thumbed a few dirt clods off his Bronco. "My parents aren't around much, but when they are, I tell them the truth, Paisley. Their reaction is their problem. And I'd never lie to my grandfather. But they'd all freak if I snuck around like you Tillery girls."

"Yeah, well, everybody's different."

Lacey rounded the back of the Bronco. "Damn. I feel better." Her blond hair fell across half her face. The curls hung in heavy mats, and her shirt was still buttoned wrong.

I could not stand seeing her like that anymore. "Lacey, do something about your shirt."

"Oh . . ." Then, right there in front of Paradise—who she didn't even know—Lacey unbuttoned her shirt. In a flashing of cleavage and lace, she realigned the ruffles and buttoned it back.

Paradise shifted his green eyes from Lacey back to me. "Everybody is different."

Lacey spun on her heels, stretched out her arms for balance. "I'm gettin' in the Bug, Paisley. You drive."

I buried my face in my hands.

I stood there waiting on Paradise to say something, anything, but he stayed silent. "Look, um"—I watched Lacey weave her way to the car—"I appreciate everything. And I'm sorry about the mud on your Bronco but your accordion's OK, and if there's a fine for the MIP and not just community service, I'll help pay for it and I'll help pay to get your car detailed."

"I got all that covered." He gave me Lacey's keys but held on to my hand. "Just so you know, I'm staying in the band."

"That's Waylon's decision. It's his band."

His fingers clasped around mine, squeezing the keys and the silver heart chain between us. I stared at my hand in his. The smooth heart pressed into the soft center of my palm. His fingers warm. His fingertips rough on the back of my hand.

"I'll be at the hangar on Monday," Paradise insisted. "You guys don't have time to find another lead singer between now and Texa-palooza."

"True." I heard the water in the creek rushing under the bridge. "Look, I know you tried to help by getting me out and that counts for something. You even got Cal out." I let my fingers close around his. "But the band depended on you. You gave us a reason not to trust you."

"I'll still be there on Monday," he said.

"What, what makes you think you can do that, just show up?"

"Because, Paisley"—he pulled me into his chest and whispered in my ear—"you're not letting go."

GRAB MY GUITAR AND RUN

Left the barn party in a flash
Saw the law, hauled ass
Hid down by the fence
No money for bail
Couldn't land in jail
Couldn't pay no stupid fine
A sheriff with a shotgun left me no choice but to grab my
    guitar and run.

I went back thinkin' you'd need me
Yeah, right, you showed me
You and Gabe had it under control
No reason to stay
I'm used to walking away
My bad, I should've seen the sign
I risked it all for you, but I still had time to grab my
    guitar and run.

I play 24/7
Rockin' hard and shreddin'

Making this Gibson scream
No chance in hell
I'll let my star plans fail
I'm firing for the sun
That dream could've come undone
So I had no choice but to grab my
    guitar and run.

11

AFTER MIDNIGHT

Lacey stumbled and bumped her way through the dark living room as if she'd been blindfolded and spun round. I made sure she was at least halfway down the hall and angling for her bedroom before I turned back to face my father. I knew he'd wait up on us. Dim amber light from a small lamp drifted from the kitchen and thickened the air with a maple syrup glow.

I sucked in a deep breath.

In the middle of the kitchen table, a cake fancied up with shredded coconut and bearing a wicked resemblance to the decapitated head of the Easter Bunny rested on a silver tray.

Dad stared at me from across the table. He took a sip of coffee, seemed to hold it in his mouth, then swallowed. "Rough movie?"

"Something like that," I said.

I dropped my head. Assessed my boots. Red mud from the depths of Tucker soil clung to the edges and heels in thick clumps.

He didn't have to say a word. We both knew I wasn't at a movie. But he'd never call me on it, which made the lying weigh even heavier on me. Maybe that was his strategy.

I wanted to look him in the eyes, straight up tell him the truth. But right now, as much as I loved him, I just couldn't trust him. Texapalooza was too close. I'd have to wait till it was over. Wait until he'd have all summer to work on my mother.

Dad's shirt was off. The jagged, red scar across his left shoulder—his throwing shoulder—reminded me that sometimes there's a price to pay for chasing a dream.

12

RESURRECTION SUNDAY

Easter Sunday morning at Cowboy Church, we strutted in late and took our seats toward the side near the cattle chutes—leftover reminders that the church had once been a livestock auction barn.

A few of the women from the center section shifted in their chairs and cut their eyes at us.

I whispered to Mother, "We're showing too much cleavage."

Mother rolled her eyes and sat up straight. Chest out.

I fidgeted with the fancy stitching on the hem of my dress. In what must have been a fairy-godmother-inspired fit, Mother had designed and sewn our Easter frocks—silk halter dresses in pastel colors cinched tight at the waist.

Mother's dress matched the purple iris she had picked for the flowering of the cross. Mine was sky blue. Lacey's soft green created a silhouette for her sallow, hungover skin. She leaned against me, her clammy cheek resting on my bare shoulder. Lacey hadn't said much when we were getting dressed other than, *God, Paisley, get me a Gatorade or I'm gonna hurl.*

Thank God for Cowboy Church. They evangelized the cowboy way with a rodeo every Friday night and a horse trough for baptizing.

If we were going to look like Wild West saloon girls, we'd at least shown up at the right ministry.

Where some churches had carved railings to mark off the altar, the Prosper County Cowboy Church had a rough-hewn fence made from cedar posts. And it was from behind the fence railing that the Slider Brothers Bluegrass and Gospel Show were about to raise Jesus from the dead.

Waylon played with his family's band. I hoped to catch him after church, let him know that Lacey and I made it . . . let him know that I'd open the hangar up for practice Monday afternoon. Maybe put in a good word for Paradise.

Like the sharp, shrill call from a hawk, a fiddle cut through the congregation. Lacey jerked herself upright. One of Waylon's uncles, decked out in an angel white, rhinestone Nudie suit and pure white Stetson, tore through a fiddle solo.

"Welcome. Welcome." Our preacher, a tall skinny man in starched Wranglers, took the stage beside the Sliders as Waylon's uncle raked the bow across the strings to a finish. "Ain't no organ in Cowboy Church. Can I get an amen on that one?" Then he took off his hat and began to pray, "Lord, on this Easter morning, we pray that you will awaken us like you awaken the wildflowers and the animals of the forest each spring. Let our hearts be resurrected, brought into a newness of life so that we may feel and see all that you have created for us to enjoy."

Lacey never bowed her head in church. Prayer time was her opportunity to scour the congregation for man candy. And thanks to the Sliders, she was good and awake—feeling and seeing all the Lord created.

Lacey elbowed me. "Hot dude. Eight o'clock. Checking you out."

Lacey used clock hands to pinpoint directions. Noon was always directly in front of us. Eight o'clock would be to my left about three rows back.

I turned around.

Paradise sat with his arms stretched across the seat backs and his hat tilted low over his forehead. He wasn't praying either.

I whipped back around just as the preacher said amen and the Sliders launched into a banjoed-up tune about being washed in the blood of the Lamb. The congregation jumped to their feet, clapping along to the Sliders' toe-tapping gospel celebration of the slaughtered Lamb.

I pretended to straighten the skirt of my dress, stealing a glance behind me. Paradise stood in dark jeans and a starched white button-down with a fistful of bluebonnets and Indian paintbrushes in his right hand as if he'd just reached down and plucked them from their roots. In that moment—in the clapping and praise singing and bluegrass-breakdown Easter service—I couldn't seem to take my eyes off him. And the rising beat in my chest—*poom-Pa, poom-PA, POOM-PA*—drowned out the common-sense voices in my head reminding me that he was an egotistical jerk who messed up the band and my chance at drumming at Texapalooza. Still, I wondered what it would feel like to press more against him than just one hand in his.

Paradise stood next to a short, silver-haired man whose skin shined as rich and dark as molasses. *The Colombian* vallenato *king*. It had to be him.

Mother leaned toward me, kept her arms folded at her waist—making it clear that she was not participating in the gospel hoedown.

"Pay attention, girls," she chimed. "They're one 'Praise Gloryland' from singing in tongues."

Lacey and I stared at her. Mother was the color commentator of Cowboy Church.

Wearing a sparkly suit that matched his fiddle-playing brother's, Waylon's father lit up his banjo and blistered the faithful in the first row.

I gripped the back of the chair in front of me, closed my eyes. I tried not to think about Paradise or the band. I wanted to get lost in the music. At first I just tapped along, barely touching the chair back with my fingertips. There was a whole range of colorful beats the Sliders' drummer could've added. A grace note. A fill. Somehow my finger tapping stretched into open slap strokes on the back of the chair.

"PAISLEY," Mother barked into her fist as if she were coughing; then she reached down and squeezed my wrist.

I stopped.

Just. Like. That.

It was like she'd shook me awake from a wonderful dream.

The Sliders stayed in high gear, rolling from one hallelujah song right into the next. I halfway expected a square dance on the altar. Waylon stood behind his father and uncle in a black suit and black tie like the other supporting band members. Nothing special. Just background. But Waylon must've gotten lost in the music too. He charged up his electric guitar on one particular song, and when the song hit its crescendo, Waylon let loose, shredding a Holy Ghost–inspired riff that lifted my heels right off the floor. I swear I could've walked on water.

I wanted to shout out and clap for the power of that music, for him. Waylon was better than his uncles. And the way he held his shoulders back when he played, popped his chest out like a proud rooster, I felt deep down he knew it too. But before Waylon could hook another chord, his father turned around and fired off a banjo smackdown that cut Waylon off at the knees. He quieted his guitar and sank back. It wasn't his show. Never would be.

Mother's not wanting me to play the drums had nothing to do with whether or not I had the talent. Waylon's struggle was different. His father showered him with high-dollar guitars and a whole mess of criticism. Waylon had the impossible task of proving himself good enough, and in the Slider family, *star* was already spoken for. For Waylon, Texapalooza was his shot at respect. Or shame. Waylon had a lot to lose, and I wasn't sure given his family pressure to be perfect I'd be able to get him to take a second chance on letting Paradise back in the band. Waylon needed a sure thing. No way would he risk a loose cannon.

I looked back at Paradise. He held the wildflowers in a white-knuckled grip and looked like he wanted to punch something. I think he might've realized for the first time what the band meant to Waylon. Maybe Paradise was mad at himself for doing to Waylon what Waylon's family had done to him for years—throwing a shadow over him. Or maybe Paradise was just mad because he wasn't up there throwing down some ego-propping performance.

Little clouds of gold, iridescent pollen danced around the windows in the Sunday morning light. I hadn't heard a word the preacher said, but I understood spring and resurrection and new beginnings. I knew the best chance for all our dreams was a fresh start. And I knew that I had to persuade Waylon to give Paradise another shot with the band.

Paradise was right. I wasn't letting go.

"If y'all would come forward a row at a time," the preacher announced, "we'll have the flowerin' of the cross."

A wooden cross, taller than my daddy and wrapped tightly in chicken wire, leaned against the pulpit. The first-row folks filed one by one to the cross and tucked a fresh flower into the chicken wire. With each flower tucked—from bluebonnets to azaleas to dogwood blooms, even the occasional pine sprig—the crude cross transformed into a beautiful and brightly colored bouquet. That meant something to me. That something could change if you just kept at it. Stayed the course. Maybe I'd be able to pull off a change in Mother. Maybe she'd eventually see my passion for drumming, and all the work and practice, and believe right along with me.

But I was going to need more success than first chair in the school band and ones at solo and ensemble competition for that to happen. Texapalooza was as critical to me as it was to Waylon. If we could do well there, Mother would have proof in front of her that I was serious. We were serious. The band was more than just a bunch of no-direction slackers headed for trouble.

Our row filed toward the cross. For most folks, this was a reverent and sacred event. For Mother, it was a red carpet.

When I stepped into the aisle, Paradise rolled his shoulders as if a gust of spring wind had just spirited up his shirt. There was no part of me he wasn't taking in, and he made no attempt to hide that fact. I tried to cover my cleavage with my daffodil. Lacey had a pink tulip tucked behind her ear. If Jesus showed up, he'd sure have his work cut out for him.

I placed my daffodil onto the cross. Waylon watched, and I

could tell from the way he raised his eyebrows that he wanted to know if Lacey and I were in trouble. I grinned. Shook my head. When I turned around, Mother glared at me as though I'd just struck some soul-swapping deal with the devil. I laughed to myself at the notion that she might think that Waylon and I were into each other. I could almost see the wheels of worry starting to turn in her head.

With no flower to hold and trying not to hobble in my heels, I put my shoulders back and owned my walk down the aisle.

Paradise cocked that dimpled little grin of his.

When church was over, Dad shook hands and fielded questions about the upcoming major-league baseball season. Even though he played professionally only a short time, Dad was still the local expert and celebrity. His fame gave Mother the opportunity to collect compliments and brag on her dressmaking.

Lacey and I waited in the gravel parking lot by the metal statue of a cowboy kneeling in front of a cross. April was the wrong month for halter dresses, and I shivered in the cool spring air.

"Well, praise the Lord." Lacey quit rubbing her arms and clasped her hands in front of her like a sweet little church girl. "I do believe the Holy Spirit is upon us."

Paradise, with the older man beside him, walked toward us. I had never really noticed before, but Paradise had a slight bow in his legs—sort of like the eye of a needle—just enough room to slip a hand between.

"He's in the band, Lacey." I tried to stand firm on the gravel, but wasn't very sure-footed in platform heels. "And it was his Bronco that I drove out last night. You should apologize. You basically peed in front of him."

The sound of gravel crunching grew louder. Paradise stopped beside me.

"Paisley, meet my grandfather."

The old man, half the size of Paradise, smiled as he held my hand. "I am Javier Cordova and you are the little drummer girl."

Lacey snickered.

"Gabriela tells me you are very good."

"Thank you." I really didn't appreciate being referred to as "the little drummer girl," but it was impossible not to be nice to the man. He had an insulating sweetness about him.

"Gabriela is going to be an accordion king. It is his destiny."

And with that announcement, he might as well have placed a heavy weighted robe with all the hope and promise that an aging king could possibly have in his offspring on Paradise's shoulders. Paradise twisted the heel of his boot, grinding the gravel into a powder.

His grandfather continued, "He is the best I've ever seen. And I have seen Alejo Durán. We are so proud Gabriela has found a band and can play." With that he nodded and walked off.

Paradise stared across the parking lot, seemingly over and beyond the tops of the tallest pines. Paradise was hardly different from Waylon. Waylon had the pressure of not being good enough to carry on the family name. Paradise had all the pressure that comes with the expectation to be great. Neither wanted to disappoint.

"Isn't Gabriela a girl's name?" Lacey asked out of the blue, oblivious to the weight of his grandfather's words.

"It's Colombian. Nothing girl about it." Paradise reached out and touched the silk bow tying my halter dress together. "I'm guessing the Easter-egg-colored dresses weren't your idea?"

Lacey stared at me. Her eyes as wide as if she'd just witnessed a miracle.

"I put in an order," I lied.

"I wasn't saying I didn't like it."

I wobbled in my high heels. "Thanks for bringing your grandfather by. He's sweet."

"I wasn't bringing him by. You were on the way." Paradise took the keys out of his pocket. His blue Bronco, sparkling from a fresh wash and with the hard top off, was not more than fifteen feet from where we stood. "See you tomorrow at rehearsal." He took a few slow steps backward before turning around and walking off.

Lacey began waving at Waylon. "Waylon!"

Waylon stomped up with his guitar slung over his shoulder. He looked like a man who'd lost his mojo.

"Waylon, you were awesome." Lacey loved to hear Waylon play as much as anyone. "You're the only reason I didn't fake the flu and stay home this morning."

Waylon hugged Lacey like she was the best big sister ever. "Paisley, I'll see you tomorrow at the hangar. I'll figure out what we're going to do about a lead singer."

I mustered up a compliment. He needed one. "Lacey's right, Waylon. You're awesome. After Texapalooza, everyone will know it too." We stood for a minute, and I thought about hugging him. But it was Waylon, and I still remembered when he told everyone in third grade that I ate dog food like popcorn. So no hugging. I gave him a sympathy rub on his arm.

Mother snuck up and pointed at him with her patent-leather clutch bag. "Well, Waylon, isn't there a big Slider tour bus you should be on?" She kept flipping the gold-and-rhinestone clasp on the bag. *Snip-snap. Snip-snap.*

I moved my hand off his arm. Waylon left.

"Paisley, there better not be anything more to what I just saw," Mother threatened.

A sudden blast of accordion music filled the parking lot. Paradise, his hat off and his hair blowing in the rush of wind, left the parking lot in the key of G.

Little did Mother know, Waylon was the least of her worries.

GRASS CLIPPIN' THINKIN'

You ever mowed grass? I'm bettin' you haven't.
    It'll screw with your mind
    Hearin' a Snapper whine
    Doin' yard-mowin' time
    Grass clippin'. Mind trippin'.

I worked three days this week mowin' yards after school
    The sun beat down
    I'd make another round
    Grass clippin'. Mind trippin'.

I see you checkin' out Gabe, your eyes don't lie
    What's so damn great
    About a beefed-up guy?
    Grass clippin'. Mind trippin'.

I grabbed a cold drink, sat down, tried to think
    Don't we want the same things?
    He gets the heat.
    I get the sweet.
    Grass clippin'. Mind trippin'.

13

THE HOLDUP

Come Monday, Uncle L. V. was kicked back in a lawn chair on his patio, soaking up some late afternoon sun. He had his feet propped up on a cooler and a gallon tub of Blue Bell Homemade vanilla in his lap. He raised one foot, pulled a bottle of Shiner Bock from the cooler, and popped the cap off with his teeth.

I sat down on the cooler and held out a paper plate with a piece from our Easter cake on it. "I brought you an ear, but it doesn't look like you need any more carbs."

"All things in moderation, Paisley. Includin' moderation." L. V. leaned forward and lifted the plastic wrap. "Bet she spent all day dying that coconut pink." He took the spoon from his ice cream and cut the bunny ear in half. He dropped it in the ice cream tub.

I watched him chew. His door-knocker mustache had a life of its own; it reminded me of a little furry gerbil. "I also put some honey-glazed ham and peas in your refrigerator. I didn't think you'd be here. That rain Saturday night keep you from flying?"

L. V. swallowed a big bite of cake and ice cream, then washed it down with the beer. "Flyin' in the rain's easy. It's the takin' off and landin' in it that gets complicated." He leaned back, flipped his ponytail over the chair, and closed his eyes. "Paisley, there are old pilots. There are bold pilots. But there ain't any old bold pilots."

The high-pitched squeal from Cal's Gibson guitar floated toward us. I took note of Waylon's old Camaro and Levi's truck parked behind the hangar. No sign of Paradise's Bronco.

L. V. opened one eye. "I guess that worried look means y'all ain't makin' Texapalooza?"

"We've got to make it." I walked to the edge of the patio, looked toward the blacktop road. "It's the biggest high school band showcase anywhere, but it's eighteen and under. Levi and our new lead singer are probably both eighteen." I turned back to L. V. "This is our shot. Waylon's paid the entrance fee. Do or die."

"So other than my sister"—L. V. took another swig of beer—"what's the hold up?"

Coming in the distance, up the long drive to L. V.'s house, the distinctive sound of Carlos Vives filled the afternoon. The baby blue Bronco, still topless, rolled to a stop between the house and the hangar. Paradise put his hat on his head and stepped out. He smiled at me as he threw on a flannel shirt.

"Oh Lord, Paisley." L. V. shook his head—half laughing, half beer-sipping. "You've got yourself a problem."

Paradise walked up and shook hands with L. V. "Gabriela Grenados."

"L. V., this would be our lead singer." I kept the introduction short, hoping L. V. wouldn't read anything more into it than he already had. "And he plays the accordion."

L. V. planted a hard stare on Paradise, giving him the once-over from the tip of Paradise's snip-toe boots, to the rips in his jeans, to the small gold loops in each ear. L. V. took a swig of his beer, then asked, "Zydeco or *vallenato*?"

Paradise smiled, but I don't think L. V. noticed his dimple.

I could've dropped a dime in it.

"*Vallenato*," Paradise said and stretched an even bigger grin. "My grandfather's a Colombian accordion king."

"Then you wear his hats and leave mine alone."

Paradise kept his chin up. "Yes, sir."

L. V. pointed his beer at him. "I'm guessing your family's got something to do with that new coffee-roasting plant being built in Jessup County."

"We import coffee." Paradise fidgeted with his leather bracelet. "My father didn't want his coffee beans to have to travel so far from the port in Houston, so we moved here from Paradise."

"Son." L. V. chuckled and smoothed his mustache with his thumb and index finger. "I've been all over this state. You didn't move from Paradise. You moved to it."

As much as Mother loathed Prosper County, Uncle L. V. loved it. He'd been all over the world, but he always came home as if home was the place that strengthened him. I started walking toward the hangar before L. V. schooled us on East Texas history and before he could ask what in the heck Paradise was doing in his house with me. "We've got a lot of work to do and not so much daylight."

Paradise followed behind me to the hangar.

"Paisley," he called out.

I kept walking.

I'd been thinking about what I'd say, to him, to Waylon. But there wasn't anything to say. We needed to play and move on. No point trying to get Paradise to make a blood oath not to use us as his backup band.

"Paisley!"

Blood oath or not we were going to have to trust him. The way I figured it, we all just needed to practice and get better and hopefully by the time we took the stage in Austin, we'd be ready and we'd play as the Waylon Slider Band.

When I rounded the corner by the hangar, Paradise ran behind me and snatched my drumsticks from my back pocket.

I whipped around, marching him backward against the hangar. I held my hand out. "You're really good at making stupid choices."

"I need to talk to you before we go in," he said, holding the sticks above his head out of my reach.

"See, that's where you're wrong. None of us in the band need to talk to you. We need to trust you. And right now, you've just stolen my drumsticks. I'm not feeling real trusty."

Paradise rolled the drumsticks between his fingers and bent his arm just enough to make his biceps swell. "You can't expect me just to sing lead then fade into the background."

I laughed. "Yeah, well, none of us expect you and your accordion to fade into the background. It's all about you, *Gabriela*, and that's the problem."

"I'll do what I have to, to be a part of the band. You've got my word." Paradise extended the drumsticks to me; then he pulled them back.

"You trust me?" He dangled the sticks.

I reached for them. He pulled them away.

"Say you trust me."

"I don't trust you." I jumped to grab at the sticks and missed.

Paradise laughed. "I took an MIP for you, for the others. You know I'm not going to mess the band up again. I'm not giving the sticks back until you admit that you can trust me."

I snatched his hat off his head. "Now what?"

Paradise grabbed me around the waist, picking me up off the ground. He slipped the drumsticks and his hand into the back pocket of my shorts. And he kept it there, holding me to him with his other hand pressing against my back. His breath warmed my neck. His hair, or maybe it was a hint in the breeze, smelled like the wisteria in full bloom and tangled in the treetops. My lips touched his ear and I just held on—breathing, taking him all in. "Put me down."

From the corner of my eye, I could see L. V. standing on his patio, watching every move we made.

"You need to move your hand." I stretched my legs toward the ground.

Paradise set me down.

I clutched his hat to my chest. "It's really Waylon that has to trust you."

14

LEVI LAYS IT ON THE LINE

Levi was not himself.

I expected a fair amount of resistance from Waylon, but I never gave one thought to Levi. The band was only a side thing for him. Levi had colleges beating his door down with baseball offers. Furthermore, he was dipping. Levi hadn't been dipping since last summer when Lacey told him it was gross and girls would never kiss him because he'd get a black, hairy fungus on his tongue. Still, the wintergreen stench of chewing tobacco hung inside the hangar.

Cal must have taken the tarp off my drums. They were uncovered and it was like him to be so thoughtful.

"I guess we can get started," I announced. With Paradise beside me, I decided to put everything on the line. Go for broke. "We're all here." I hoped the pretend-like-the-disaster-at-the-Tucker-Barn-never-happened approach would fly.

It never got off the ground.

Waylon was leaving. He stripped off his guitar and kicked open its case.

"Waylon." I knelt down and closed the case before he could put away his guitar. "Let it go. We've got to have him."

"You may, but I don't. I can go to Nashville and play backup right now, right this minute, for anyone. I'm not playing backup in my own band." Waylon faced Paradise, turning his nose up as if he smelled roadkill. "He's . . . he's using you, Paisley."

Paradise rolled his sleeves up. He obviously took that personally, and I wasn't sure if he was distracting himself with the sleeve rolling or prepping for a fight. Furthermore, given what just happened outside the hangar, that remark kicked me in the gut. But if Paradise was using me, then Waylon was too. "Look around, Waylon. You're in my uncle's hangar. What does that mean you're doing?"

Waylon's guitar case was easy enough for him to reach down and pick up, but he wasn't moving on it.

"We're all using each other," I explained. "It's not such a bad thing."

"It's Waylon's band, Paisley." Levi stood up with his bass resting on the tip end of his work boot. He spit a brown tobacco-juice zinger into a Dixie cup and glared at Paradise. "Dude, I ain't got no problem with you or your squeezebox. I'll even give you some points for helping Paisley and Lacey and Cal get home. But if you're hung up on bein' an attention whore, you can hang a tambourine off your left foot and be your own one-man band. Make no mistake. We will walk offstage and leave your ass up there." *Thooooop.* He nailed a brown spit wad in the cup again.

We all stood stock-still like mannequins. Immobile. Reverent. Even Cal, who was always fingering a chord, silenced his Gibson. From the nose of the old bomber, *Miss Molly Moonlight*'s come-hither-honey grin morphed into a gasp of pure shock.

"Levi." I reached out to touch his arm, but he turned away.

He set his cup down on the hangar floor, gripped his bass guitar by the neck. "Y'all know I'm done after Texapalooza. But if that's off, then I'm done now."

Levi pulled in his bottom lip; the muscles in his cheeks jumped. He wouldn't look at me. Whatever was bothering him had to run deeper than band issues with Paradise or Texapalooza.

Paradise stepped up. "I got carried away, man." He slapped Levi on the back. "Must've been your home brew."

Levi ignored Paradise and locked eyes with Waylon.

"It won't happen again," Paradise added.

I liked to be able to count on things: the sun coming up, even Mother's dependable disapproval of my heathen drum dreams. I'm a planner and I count on the constants in my life. Levi's good-humored swagger had been a certainty for as long as I could remember. It wasn't like him to snap, cuss, and dip in a single hot-tempered moment.

Cal Boone, God love him, started plucking a plinky-sounding kid's tune. I swear it was the Barney song. *I love you. You love me.*

Levi rolled his eyes, but his jolly heart wanted to laugh. I could see it.

I took that opening to scoot across the concrete. Get behind my drums. Change the momentum.

Waylon futzed around like a kid pacing on a high board, getting ready to dive for the first time. Finally, he pulled his guitar over his shoulder and turned to me. "Count us in on four."

Four was Waylon's blues-rock count. I let the sticks speak the rhythm. One. Two. One, two, three, four. Waylon was testing Paradise with one of Waylon's own signature songs.

Paradise left his accordion in his murse. If Waylon was going to test him, Paradise was committed to passing. He managed to put his pride to the side for the sake of the band. That scored points with me.

Paradise waited for Waylon to open the song, let him carve the intro with an unmistakable wailing that only his skill and his '61 Fender Stratocaster could pull off.

I kept the beat steady, held the song together, barely hitting the snare on the backbeat. Slow and simple. That was the blues. That and locking in with the bass player.

But Levi still wouldn't look at me.

Not that it mattered so much musically. We'd played together, played Waylon's songs so much that we knew to simply anchor the groove. I suppose we didn't have to look at each other. But that didn't change the fact that we always did. That's when I knew whatever Levi's problem was, it had something to do with me.

Paradise must've practiced at home because when Waylon turned the song over to him, Paradise growled out Waylon's lyrics in his velvety bass. The more he sang, the more his voice melted with the whining guitars, the more the deep drum tones seemed to sink like an anchor in a dark sea, the worse I felt about Levi.

We played it out, song after song, according to Waylon's playlist, like we should've done at the Tucker Barn. After about the fifth song, Paradise added his accordion. He drew out the bellows, which howled through the hangar like a lonesome train whistle. No rocking Carlos Vives. Paradise proved he could fall in with the Waylon Slider Band.

I rode the blues tempo—rode it from one song to the next and into the next, as smooth and slow as the sun setting over the pasture. Feeling my heart drop on every ghost note. I had to figure out exactly what Levi's problem was.

Uncle L. V. stepped into the hangar just as we finished. "Y'all plannin' on depressin' everyone in Austin?" He pointed his beer at Cal's guitar. "Or are you gonna let him use that Gibson on some Southern rock?"

Waylon smiled for the first time. L. V. had ridden him for months about going wide-open and not playing so much in his daddy's style. "We worked the slow stuff today. We don't have much time left."

Levi packed up his bass. "We practicing again this week, Waylon?" He said it like he had a thousand things to do and needed to get rehearsal on the calendar. But Levi had never been a calendar kind of guy.

Waylon glanced at me, then appealed to L. V. "We're behind the eight ball. We've got to pull together a fifteen-minute set that shows our style and still gives each of us a chance to show what we can do individually. We're going to start . . ."

L. V. waved him off as Waylon launched into one of his overly detailed explanations. "Use the hangar anytime, son." L. V. turned to me. "Make it work, Paisley. But your momma ain't ever going to believe my house needs cleaning more than once a week."

Levi slammed the lid on his guitar case. "Call me when you figure rehearsal out, Waylon." He stomped toward the hangar door.

I tucked my sticks in my back pocket and ran out after him. I still had daylight left to burn. "Levi, stop."

Levi dropped his guitar in his truck bed then opened the door.

"Levi, what is wrong with you?" I stared up at him. "Please tell me what I did."

"I ain't lying for you anymore, Paisley. That goes for Lacey too."

"Lying? I don't understand." I glanced beyond his truck. Clover had gone to seed and the blush across the pasture matched the red in Levi's cheeks. "I've never asked you to lie for me."

Levi reached into the door pocket and pulled out a can of Skoal. "Not directly." He pinched a fresh wad and tucked it behind his bottom lip. "Paisley, I have to face your daddy every day at the batting cages. Jack Tillery taught me to pitch. He caught balls for me when no one else had the guts to get behind the plate. He's the reason for my scholarships." Levi spit a dart at the ground. "I'm going to college because of him. No one in my family's ever done anything more than a few hours at community college. If it weren't for baseball, if it weren't for your daddy, I don't know what I'd be doin'."

I heard Paradise's accordion rip through the hangar. L. V. and Waylon and Cal were taking him to task. "I've never asked you to lie for me, Levi. Me or the band."

"Your daddy knows. He ain't stupid." Levi spit again. "He knows about the band. He knows about the parties. God, Paisley. He asked me at the cages this afternoon if I was takin' care of you and Lacey." When Levi wiped his cheek with his big bear paw of a hand, I thought I'd crumble. "I should've stepped up sooner. I let Coach Till down. I let Lacey down. I can't stand what she's doin' to herself."

I knew he meant all of it. I also knew how he felt about Lacey. He'd always wanted to date her, but he had the absolute worst of résumés in my mother's mind: a deeply rooted East Texas country boy and a baseball player. He was everything Mother stayed hell-bent on keeping us from.

Levi took a long study of his red-dirt-stained boots. "I may not be the sharpest knife in the drawer, but I know this: A lie ain't no rifle bullet. It's a shotgun shell. You and Lacey think you're lying to your momma and gettin' around her. Truth is, there's a whole lot of other people gettin' hit when you pull that trigger."

"You know how my mother is." I half resented Levi trying to make me out to be the bad girl in this situation. "There'd be no drums, no band, no nothing for me if she knew the truth."

Levi stepped into his truck and sat behind the wheel. "That's what you keep sayin', and Lacey keeps sayin' she wouldn't get to go to beauty school. But neither one of you have given Diane Tillery a chance to be that big of a bitch."

My mouth fell open. Levi was serious.

He kept on, "And neither one of you have bothered to trust your own daddy to help."

Now I was ticked. "So what do you suggest I do? March down to my house and tell my mother about the band and that we're rehearsing every day until Texapalooza, which by the way I'm also going to play at? How about that? Is that what you think?"

"Yep."

"You should've stopped with your own admission that you're not the sharpest mind around."

"Maybe so, Paisley." He turned his head and stared through the truck windshield. He whispered, "But at least I'm not a liar."

"I can't tell my mother the truth. Not yet. But I will soon. I plan on telling everyone, after Texapalooza." Whether Levi was right or not didn't matter. I had my reasons. He knew that. "Don't judge me because . . ."

Levi held up his hand. He didn't care about my reasons. "It'll be a lot worse if she finds out before you get a chance to tell her."

Levi cranked his truck and slammed the door. The window was down. "I told Coach Till I was a grown-ass man, and I wasn't hidin' my feelings for Lacey anymore. I told him I wanted to ask Lacey out. He said I could and that he'd talk to Diane." Levi put the truck in gear and started down the drive. "You should try the truth sometime."

15

MOTHER CAN'T HANDLE
THE TRUTH

It was taco night, and Mother had decorated the table in Fiesta-ware—a dizzying display of blue and yellow and red and green.

I wasn't sure which was sweating more—my glass of tea or me. I had made up my mind to tell Mother about the band. I'd weighed it and decided that maybe Levi was right and I should give her a chance. And deep down, I felt my daddy would stand behind me.

"Paisley, you look sick." Mother set a bowl of black beans beside me. "Have you been breathing in bleach? You know you've got to raise the windows for ventilation when you're cleaning."

Lacey chimed in, "Paisley, tell us if you're huffing mildew remover. We're here to help." She faked a concerned sniffle, and her gypsy bracelets jingled when she put her hand over her heart. "Cowboy Church offers a Wednesday night class on addiction, you know. The first step in getting help is admitting you have a problem."

I knew she was joking, but I considered catapulting a spoonful of beans at her. "You're in an awfully good humor." I decided to get her back. "How are those tryouts for the Singing Eagles coming along?"

Lacey took that on the chin. She even smiled this evil little grin, like she had everything under control.

Mother answered for her. "Tryouts begin next week. Lacey is locked in." Mother opened the tortilla warmer and steam plumed in the air. "She has so much more, *much more* performance experience than some of those wannabes. I'm sure."

Lacey rolled a tortilla full of meat and cheese. She cut her eyes at Dad. Mother wasn't the only one who had something cooking for dinner.

Dad took a big swig of tea; he softly set the glass down, rubbing the side with his thumb. "I talked to that youngest Tucker boy today."

I spun my fork between my fingers. This was it. Dad was about to spring the whole Levi and Lacey situation on Mother. Lacey knew it too.

Mother cackled. "Was he sober and standing upright?"

"Diane." Dad leaned back in his chair, clasped his hands behind his head like he didn't have a thing to hide. "Levi's all right. He's not planning on staying around and working the vineyard."

Mother interrupted, "Growing a few grapes does not turn a generational bootleg operation into a winery."

"He's got scholarship offers coming in from all over—even the university."

Dad let that soak in.

"Stop that annoying thumping, Paisley." Mother stared at my fork. I had gone from spinning it to rocking it back and forth against my plate in a *ping-pong, ping-pong* rhythm.

"Well, goody goody for Mr. Levi Tucker," Mother continued. "However, I'd bet the farm that he forgets all about college when that first major-league team offers him a nickel."

Dad scooted his plate back and took another drink of tea. Mother's remark stung him. She measured everyone, everything against her own experiences. And she'd convinced herself that being rural was an obstacle and that a promise of money trumped academic goals any day of the week.

"Times are different now than they were back when I was—when we were making choices, Diane. Levi's made up his mind that he's going to school. He wants an education."

Mother rolled her eyes and scooped herself some black beans.

Dad added, "And he's made up his mind that he wants to take Lacey on a date."

Sonic. Boom.

Her spoon dropped into the beans and sank to the soupy black bottom. Mother's eyes widened, and I thought her false eyelashes would stick to her eyebrows.

Dad finished, "He had the manners to come and ask me. I told him we'd approve."

"You had no right to tell him that. Lacey doesn't want to go out with the likes of him." Mother pinned her eyes on her.

Lacey's back bowed like a cornered cat.

"No, ma'am." Mother shot to her feet. "No. No. No." She marched to the stove and started clearing pots and clanging pans. "No. No, sir. No, ma'am. Not having it." Mother pounded a wooden spoon against the side of a pot, then threw it in the sink. "I bet he would like to take her out, probably try and get her drunk, knock her up." She threw a wet dishrag at Dad. "You'd approve of that too, wouldn't you?"

Lacey jumped straight up from her chair. The place mat slipped, and Mother's Mexican-themed place setting crashed to the floor in colorful ceramic chunks. So much for taco-night fiesta. The pictures lining the hall wall rattled when Lacey slammed her bedroom door.

I started to leave, follow Lacey. But I was still ripe to tell Mother about the band, get it over with. Maybe it was better if we all just rained down the truth on her at once.

Dad walked to the stove and hugged Mother from the back, around her waist. He took a skillet from her hands and kissed her cheek. He simply held her as if the strength in his arms had the power to bend her will.

Mother's voice cracked. "This is not what we've worked for with the girls. I can't turn Lacey loose with Levi Tucker. I won't do it. She's got to stay focused on her own dreams and plans. I won't have her toss it to the side and lose it all because of some boy."

That comment set my teeth on edge. I could've bit through a saddle strap. Mother threw the "some boy" remark out more than I cared to hear. No one in the house was confused that who she was really talking about was Dad. I wanted to tell her that it took both of them to make their choices, that she should back off Dad.

Dad squeezed her tighter. Her remark had to torture him, but he always managed to push past the pain. He'd lose a battle but win a war.

"You're going to have to trust me on this one," he whispered to her. Dad had an impressive amount of patience and conviction. Watching him love my mother—day in and day out—almost made me believe there was really something to the whole one-life-one-love thing. They hadn't settled for each other just to do the right thing. He loved her.

"Why the Tucker bunch, Jack?" Mother whimpered. "For crying out loud, that boy's mother holds the county distance record for watermelon seed spitting."

"Lacey wants to go out with Levi, not his mother." His lips brushed her cheek as he spoke. "She's a senior. It's time to cut her some slack."

I think they forgot I was even there. I slipped out. Mother had all the truth she could handle. Dad had all the bitterness he could hold.

16

RUB AND STROKE

I made it through the woods and up to L. V.'s just in time to see him lift off, over the tops of the pines. In the bright afternoon sun, *Miss Molly's* heavy aluminum sides flashed like mirrors in the clear blue sky. They were off. Watching *Miss Molly* defy gravity, get off the ground and soar, made me believe I could do anything. Nothing could hold me down.

"Looks like you've got the place to yourself."

I almost jumped straight out of my boots.

Paradise laughed and took a step back. "Whoa. Easy."

I pressed my hand against my heart. "Stop sneaking up on me."

Paradise kept his hands behind his back. "Last time I checked, driving up and slamming a car door, calling out your name isn't sneaking. Maybe you should blame that sky-rattling buzz coming from that tin can your uncle's flying off in."

I grinned and walked into the hangar. Paradise didn't like to fly. I could hear it in his voice whenever he mentioned L. V. and the planes. "You're early."

"Maybe I planned it that way."

He was hiding something. I zipped my hoodie. I wasn't sure what he wanted.

Or maybe I was.

The hangar was silent except for the tweeting of the sparrows nesting along the roof.

"I brought you a present." Paradise pulled a small drum not much bigger than a large coffee can from behind his back.

I reached for it, taking it from him. "It's a *caja*." I rubbed my fingertips across the drumhead.

"That's calf skin. It's traditional. This is real rope too. Not nylon." Paradise drew his finger along one of the ropes running down the side of the wooden drum. "My grandfather said if the little drummer girl is going to play *vallenato*, she needs the real deal."

"This is mine?" I patted the center as if it were a baby's bottom. *Poom-poom-poom.* I couldn't believe it. I used L. V.'s drum kit. I used the school's snare. I had never had a drum of my own. "I'm just borrowing this, right?"

"Paisley." Paradise took a deep breath. "It's a gift. Are you afraid you can't play it?"

The crazy tweeting of the birds reached a crescendo.

Paradise smiled, raising his eyebrows. Waiting.

"Thank you." I paused, listening for Waylon's or Levi's truck. Still early. I checked the open doorway to the hangar. Not a soul in sight.

I stepped toward Paradise—breathing in, breathing out, inching closer, holding the little drum between us. "Thank you." I leaned toward him.

He tucked his arm around my waist, drawing me into his chest. The beating of his heart pulsed strong against my cheek. Paradise slipped one hand along the base of my neck, just inside my shirt collar. He kissed the top of my head. "I like that there's no purity-ring promise against hugging."

"I'm not afraid to hug you." I kicked my stool out from under the tarp. "And I'm not afraid to play this drum." I sat down on the stool. "It's like a conga drum?" I held it under my arm.

Paradise laughed. His green eyes lit up like the high gloss emerald on a mallard's head. "You're tucking it like a football." He took the drum and knelt down beside me. "Hold it between your knees." He placed his hand on my knee and gently pushed my legs open, placing the drum between my thighs.

My throat tightened. The air thinned. I wished the hangar had fans. "I've got it." I pushed his hand away. "I've got it." I squeezed the drum, holding it tight between my legs.

"You do play it bare-handed," he said as he stood up. "Rub and stroke like the conga. But *meringue*, more Latin than Caribbean. You have to find the passion, feel it."

I started softly enough. Keeping it simple in two-four time, drawing the sound out instead of beating it in. There was a physical connection. Immediate. I could feel the beat all over.

Paradise opened his murse. "Not fancy, but good." He smiled as he opened his accordion.

"I'm not supposed to fancy it up," I told him. "I set the pace. I'm just the timekeeper."

"That's like saying a heart just pumps blood." Paradise opened his accordion. "You're the life of the band, Paisley." He glanced at the hangar door. The muffled rumble of Waylon's old truck drifted in.

"You're the heartbeat."

17

LACEY GOES UP IN SMOKE

The blue-and-white paisley-patterned pillow on which Mother had monogrammed a large needlepoint *P* made the best imitation drum. I might have to hide the *caja* in the hangar with the rest of the drums, but Mother wouldn't suspect a thing with pillow practicing. Sitting on the edge of my bed with the pillow between my knees, I was hard at work perfecting my slap stroke when Lacey flung the door wide.

She shut it behind her, falling against it as if someone had chased her down the hall. "That was close." She huffed and coughed.

Whatever Lacey was up to, I wanted no part of this close to Texapalooza. "You can't hide in here. I'm practicing."

Lacey's eyes darted around my bedroom. She fished her hand into her shirt and pulled a small box from her cleavage. Before I could stand, Lacey dived to the floor and slipped a pack of cigarettes under my bed. With the cigarettes safely hidden, she crawled to her hands and knees, panting and griping. "Mother never goes to the barn. She would have to pick this afternoon of all days to start planting her herb garden down there."

I reached under the bed, grabbed the pack, and hit Lacey in the chest with it. "You get those out of my room." Lacey and I hadn't had a hair-pulling throw down in years, but I was up for one. If Mother found me with cigarettes, she'd lose her mind. "Get 'em out of here, Lacey." Then it struck me. Lacey was smoking. "Wait a minute. When did you start smoking?"

Lacey fumigated herself with one of my spray bottles of perfume. "I don't smoke," she argued. "I mean, I'm not a regular. I'm situationally smoking. Only until my situation next week is over. See?" She held the cigarettes out. "No filters. I'm starting to sound like, um, who's that chick with the hair that L. V. has a poster of?"

"Stevie Nicks?"

"Yeah, whoever." Lacey fanned her hands around so that we both smelled like lavender eau de toilette. "I've been on the east side of the barn smoking like a hooker for three straight days." She coughed some more. "No way will they let me in the Singing Eagles with this jacked-up voice."

"Did Mother see you come in here?"

"Gosh no." Lacey collapsed onto the bed, her chest heaving with every labored breath. "I heard Di-*ane*—rolling a wheelbarrow full of garden crap down to the barn—I stomped out my cigarette real good—hauled ass around to the west side—ran like a roadrunner to the house."

I plopped next to her. "Lacey, you've lost it." The cigarettes lay on her chest. "You're hurting yourself."

"Reality check, Paisley. You can't talk. It's not like you aren't running your own game." Lacey twirled a long strand of hair around her finger. "And you're starting to sound like Levi."

Levi and his shotgun-blast lie theory had some merit. All the convenient truths in the world weren't worth Lacey compromising her health.

"I'm buying myself some time," she said. "You saw how Mother flipped smooth out when Dad told her Levi and I were talking. Which we are and which we will continue to do whether she likes it or not, knows about it or not." Lacey's voice had a sharp edge to it that didn't come from the cigarettes. "Paisley..." Her cheeks had cooled, but they fired back up into a throbbing scarlet. "Levi and I've been close since grade school, but something's changed this spring. Levi's taken things slow because he didn't want to make trouble with Mother. That's all out in the open now, but if she runs him off, I swear I don't know what I'll do."

Listening to Lacey, something clicked for me. Like the chambering of a gun shell. *Ka-thwump.* Locked and loaded. Getting around Mother was easy and harmless enough at first, but the lies and the secrecy were fast becoming a tangled mess. "As soon as Texapalooza is over with," I told her, "I'm laying it all out there. Everything."

"Everything, Paisley?" She grabbed my hand, touching my purity ring as if she'd once lost something special just like it. She turned my hand over, tracing my palm like a psychic. "Levi says the band thinks something's going on with you and that accordion-playing stud."

"Nothing yet."

Lacey laughed. "I know, I know. You're all about the band. But Levi says the dude is sprung where you're concerned. It's written all over his face."

My heart skipped like a single stroke roll across the toms. I could see his face—the sly-fox grin and the green eyes.

"So other than bearing gifts." Lacey grinned. Levi must've told her about the *caja*. "Has he tried anything?"

"Oh, gosh, Lacey, no." My neck heated up. "We just talk about music. The band."

Lacey tucked her cigarettes back down her shirt. "One thing leads to another," she warned. "It always does."

THE RIDER

Cruising the deep storm drain under dim street lights
A concrete buzz rolling under my wheels
Up the steep sides, gaining speed, taking flight
Bank a 180, land an acid drop.
Can't stop.

I don't shut my eyes
I train my sights
As I ride I know what's coming up ahead of me.
The world can try to steal, you may never feel
But that won't change the life I'm carving out for me.

I dig hard on the heel edge, lean in, cut and turn
A grinding screech of the deck against the concrete
Got no pearl snap shirt, no cash to be a confident flirt
My love's not sketchy, kick-flip
Heart rip.

I never shut my eyes
I keep my sights

As I ride I know what's coming up ahead of me.
The world can try to steal, you may never feel
But I see the life I'm carving out for me.

Lean

      Cut

            Turn

18

PASSION AND PERFORMANCE

Drumming in L. V.'s hilltop hangar alone—the door shut, the sparrows silent. Feeling the isolation of being so far away from towns, honking horns, and blinking red lights and the stop-and-go stop-and-go push-push-push-let-me-through racket—I split open a vein. Pumping out a beat, a pulse. Absorbing the rebound. The return. Six-stroke roll. Flam. Paraparadiddle. With the speed of a hummingbird's wings.

I couldn't remember when I first played: maybe rapping a spoon against a stainless steel pan in the kitchen or maybe riding through the pasture, standing in the bed of the pickup slapping out a tin-can tinging tune on the truck's roof. Rhythm was as much a part of who I was as red dirt and pine trees. I could ignore my passion, turn my back. But deep down the rhythm would continue to pulse with every beat of my heart. A pine tree can't lose the sharp smell of evergreen.

I rested my sticks, picked up the *caja*. The pillow practice had worked. My hand strokes drew out an earthy Latin groove that danced around the hangar. I loved the rough feel of the animal skin under my fingers and palms. The stroke and the rub. The *caja*'s wooden sides vibrated against my legs. The rhythm rolled through my body, a soul-settling vibration. My shoulders bounced. My head nodded. Paradise was right. The *caja* embodies passion.

"Practicing for your solo?" Waylon—flanked by Paradise, Cal, and Levi—stood in the doorway. I never even noticed the light breaking into the hangar when they pushed open the door.

Paradise grinned and started to strap on his accordion. "Solo?" He screwed his face into a fake puzzled look. "She's just a time-keeper."

I knew he was kidding, but the others didn't. They paused as if they expected a Mack truck to barrel through the hangar.

"Very funny." I blew him off. "Just be sure you can keep up."

Ever since Paradise showed up, Cal had taken to drinking protein shakes. He gulped down what looked to be a couple pints then switched on the amps. Waylon, clutching his '61 Strat, loosened his fingers on a B. B. King barn burner.

Levi stood in front of my drum kit, thumping my crash cymbal. "We cool?" he asked.

"Nothing's changed." I was at least going to be honest with him. Make it clear that I wasn't taking any risks of ruining my chance at Texapalooza. "I'm not saying a word to my folks until after we get back from Austin."

He gave me a fist bump. "I've asked Lacey out after Texapalooza." Levi rolled the bill of his baseball cap between his palms. "Told her I'd take her to celebrate not making the Singing Eagles."

"She wouldn't have made it anyway," Waylon blurted. He handed each of us a one-page laminated playlist of our fifteen-minute set.

"Waylon"—Levi pressed his baseball cap on his head—"don't give me a reason to bust that Strat over your head."

Waylon defended himself. "I don't mean because of Lacey's singing." He shifted his beady brown eyes toward me. "It's their mom. The choir director for the Singing Eagles told my dad she was high maintenance. That she had all kinds of suggestions about outfits and costumes and even stage props. They're a traditional choir," he clarified and hopped up on his musical high horse. "Not a glee club."

I could've stuck my head between the hi-hat cymbals and pounded away. Mother's reputation didn't embarrass me. It frustrated me. Good grief. The woman had no restraint when it came to manipulating in order to make her dreams for Lacey come true.

I pretended to read Waylon's laminated playlist. Paradise and Cal stared at me. I could feel it. Didn't. Even. Look. Up. I just wanted the conversation about my mother to end.

Waylon trekked on as if we needed for him to lay out the full story. "My dad said the choir director quit returning her phone calls because she . . ."

Levi held his hand up—cutting Waylon off in mid-sentence.

Cal carved out the intro to "Sweet Home Alabama." Paradise faced me and clapped in time with Cal. I grabbed my sticks and set the pace. Before long, I was lost in the groove. Rolling through Waylon's playlist, our official Texapalooza set. Filing Mother and the aggravation that came with her away in the back of my mind. Turning the volume down on the nagging irritation that she'd never stick her neck out for me and my dreams.

We were firing on all cylinders. Levi was back to looking at me when we locked in his bass. Cal colored the songs with his Gibson.

Waylon led the charge with his wicked, powerful playing. Paradise drawled the lyrics when he was supposed to, pumped his accordion when he got the chance. The right chance.

We kept it up, rehearsing every afternoon while L. V. was gone to the air show. I couldn't wait for him to get back. Play the set for him. We were close to audience ready and in a zone.

When I showed up Thursday afternoon, the band was all there, and Paradise was sitting on my stool, my throne. The chatter of guys laughing and talking shut down with a viselike silence the minute I walked in. Paradise patted his knee as if I should sit on it.

I didn't budge. They were all up to something.

Paradise attempted a drumroll. "I've got us a gig," he said, smiling, all proud of himself. "Saturday night. Don Caliente's Taco Bar and Cantina in Jessup County."

I'd been to the cantina a few times to eat, even made a round or two on the dance floor with Dad. But always in the early evening. They had a large back room with a wooden dance floor, and on weekends the cantina turned into a bona fide Texas dance hall and honky-tonk. Twenty-one and over.

I wondered how Paradise worked us into the gig. "We don't meet the minimum age requirement."

"All under control, Paisley." He handed me my sticks. "We're going to play early, before the bar opens in the dance hall. The equipment is all set up. You can use their drum kit."

Waylon explained, "We're fronting for the house band."

I studied Waylon and Levi and Cal. They were committed. The Waylon Slider Band was playing. The road to Texapalooza was going through Don Caliente's Cantina.

"No law breaking, Paisley. It's all good," Paradise urged. "If you can swing it."

Our success at Texapalooza depended solely on our ability to perform. The only way we had to get that right was to practice on a crowd. The cantina was deep in Jessup County. The chances of someone identifying me were slim. And I was willing to take the slim chance.

"Let's do it," I said with no real thought of how to get there. "Let's play the cantina."

19

GAMES PEOPLE PLAY

A vase the size of a championship trophy overflowed with at least two dozen long-stemmed pink and yellow roses. Ribbons in every color of the rainbow and glitter-glued with GOOD LUCK, LACEY and DON'T STOP BELIEVING billowed from an enormous bow. Dad, Mother, and Lacey silently ate their dinner, barely looking up as I slid into my seat. The clinking of forks against china reminded me of the time I played the triangle in first grade.

"I'm sure your sister would've appreciated your being here earlier," Mother cracked. She had black mascara clouds under her eyes. "As much time as you've wasted up there the last two weeks, L. V.'s hangar ought to be cleaner than a Methodist's knees."

I tried to come up with something to say to Lacey. Clearly she didn't make the Singing Eagles cut, and privately she'd be jumping for joy. Still, she'd cap all that in front of Mother. "I know there's a lot of good things in the future for you, Lacey."

Dad stared at me as he bit into a buttery roll. As certain as I was that he knew about the band, I thought Lacey's long-gone desire to sing had yet to register with him. However, given his slow grinding chewing, I got the vibe that he was quickly figuring it out.

"Y'all know what?" Lacey reached for Mother's homemade macaroni and cheese and plopped a softball-size scoop on her plate. She took a deep breath and blew out what sounded like good riddance. "Paisley is right. Lots of good things in the future." She flipped her hair over her shoulder, dabbed her dry eyes with the back of her hand, then picked up her fork. "I'm just going to try my very best to put all this disappointment behind me and trust the Lord to lead me in the direction he would have me to follow." With that, Lacey shoved a forkful of mac and cheese in her mouth—smiling while she chewed, her cheeks bulging.

Dad leaned back in his chair, raising the front legs off the floor. I actually thought he might applaud her performance. "The Lord?" He rocked his chair back and forth. "The Lord." He nodded.

Mother sniffled. "God does have bigger and better plans for you, Lacey. He does. He really does. He's given you a gift, Lacey. And the Lord will work it out."

In my opinion, the Lord was going to work out that gift in a beauty parlor.

"I know." Lacey batted her eyelashes at Mother. "I'm just going to take a few days off. Relax. Then really start thinking about next steps, you know?"

Mother nodded. Dad and I watched with fascination. Next steps for Lacey probably meant a tattoo.

"What are we doing Saturday?" Lacey asked and it cut me in two. I was counting on her to help me get to the cantina.

"No plans." Mother settled back into her chair. "I really"—Mother choked back a tear. Next steps were hard on her—"I really need to work on this herb garden I'm planting down by the barn. Jack?"

Dad stared a hole through Lacey. "Pitching lessons in the morning is all. Then I'll help you." He was talking to Mother but never took his eyes off Lacey.

"Well, since we don't have family plans, I think I could use a girls' night out. Hang out with friends, eat, take in a movie."

"A movie?" Dad all but laughed out loud. He'd figured her out. Nothing else would get by him.

Mother agreed, "A girls' night out would be good for you. I know this has been hard. Believe me I do. I really do. And plus you've had the stress of that Tucker boy panting around you like a thirsty dog."

Lacey gripped her tumbler, and I thought she would pitch her iced tea on Mother. Instead, she coolly set the glass on the place mat. "Paisley, do you have plans? Why don't you come?"

She knew I never had plans. But that was it. Levi must've told her. Lacey was my ride to the cantina and my reason for being gone Saturday night.

"Sure." I tried not to act too giddy. "I'm game."

Dad set his chair down. The legs slammed against the floor. He was hanging on until Texapalooza, but I wasn't sure how much more he would overlook before calling my hand.

20

DANCE-HALL DRAMA

The dance hall at Don Caliente's Taco Bar and Cantina had a polished-wood floor primed with a fresh sprinkling of cornmeal. Slicker than an icy sidewalk. The jukebox rocked old-school Tanya Tucker singing something about her arms staying open all night. Paradise two-stepped around the dance floor, boot scooting and sliding, clutching the waist of a push-up-bra-wearing Best Piece in Town girl. The same girl from the rodeo. Her rich black hair flowed like a thoroughbred's mane with every spin, every twirl, every swing back into his arms. I couldn't believe it. Paradise brought a date to our gig. He brought a *date*.

"Paisley, keep walking," Lacey ordered and nudged me in my back. "Don't let him know you care."

I cut across the dance floor, making a beeline for the stage. He was just a flirt. A big ol' flirt. Probably using me like Waylon said, flirting with me to stay in the band. I actually thought, I mean, I was sure he liked me.

Paradise waltzed by, his cheek pressed against her ear. I swear he was whispering. I stopped as they passed, or tried to stop. My boots slipped on the slick floor. *Wham*. I busted it. Falling hard with one leg out and the other bent. An *L*—as in loser.

I scrambled to my feet as quickly as I went down, dusted off my jeans.

Lacey tidied up my bangs with her fingers. "No one saw a thing. Forget it."

When I finally reached the stage, I felt Lacey drift from my side. She'd found Levi and they were locked in a cleavage-crushing embrace. I turned to the one thing I could count on. The drums. I brushed my hand along a cymbal. A slight *ting* rang out, a whimper. I forced myself to turn my back on the dance floor. I refused to watch them. I inventoried the drums: a full kit—the basic four piece with a kick and cymbals, positioned on an old rug for stability. I'd get out of it what I expected. The throne was just a simple stool. A simple stool with my *caja* sitting on the top. I set the little drum to the side. *"Not playing it,"* I swore.

Paradise had separated himself from dancing long enough to pay attention to the reason he was in the dance hall in the first place. He prepped his accordion, but Paradise had not separated himself from the Best Piece in Town girl. She hovered beside him on the stage with us, with the band.

"Paisley." Paradise finally noticed I was in the building. He grabbed her hand. They stood in front of the drums. I pretended to tighten the snare. "You know Estella, right? From the rodeo?"

"Not formally." If my eyes could've shot venom, he'd have been in a world of hurt. "Nice to meet you." I should've stopped there, but oh, well. "Lots of chairs around the dance floor to sit on. Not so much room on the stage."

Her eyelashes fluttered like the wings of a monarch butterfly. Estella, the Best Piece in Town girl, kissed Paradise on the cheek and took a long-legged stride off the stage.

"Relax, Paisley." Paradise acted as if he held us all in the palm of his hand. "Put it all out there. You've got this." The boy was clueless.

"Can't hear you." *Paradiddle paradiddle paraparadiddle.* I shook my head, closed my eyes, hoping that when they reopened he'd be gone.

He wasn't. Paradise took his hat off and ran his fingers through his hair. His accordion hung loosely on one shoulder. I watched the rise and fall of his chest with every breath he took.

I warmed up until Waylon circled his finger in the air for us to sound check.

"On four, Paisley." Waylon pointed at me to hit it.

We started playing. It was my worst nightmare. We sounded like a group of grade-schoolers tuning instruments—not a band that had practiced for months. No one was together.

Waylon waved his arms. I thought for a minute he might just take flight. "Do it again." His face, even his ears were red.

I pounded us in on four. *BAMBAMBAMBAM.*

Paradise tapped the toe of his boot, concentrating on it, shaking his head as if the beats were all wrong. Levi moved closer to me, trying to lock in his bass. They were off. We sounded like a junkyard band. I added a three-stroke roll . . . because I felt like it.

Cal quit playing.

Waylon put his hands on his hips, sucking in deep breaths. "Paisley, you're rushing it."

I clinched my sticks in my hand and yelled at him, "Keep up, Waylon!"

The crowd, the folks in the cantina, shifted in their chairs. Their silence sent an awkward vibe onto the stage.

Paradise stared at the ceiling rafters. "Time is your job."

"Yes, I know that. But I set the pace, remember?" I stood to my feet, sweat beading around my forehead. He must've conveniently forgotten about the whole Paisley-you're-the-heartbeat-of-the-band nonsense. I couldn't have cared less about the staring crowd.

Cal slumped over a speaker.

Levi said, "You're not setting the same pace we practiced."

"Maybe so." I was burning hot. "But it's the only pace I've got right now."

Waylon sat on a stool then stood back up. Sat down and stood up. Sat down, stood up three, maybe four times. Paradise turned to Estella. More head shaking.

Of all the whack-ass times to try and get my attention, Lacey pointed at Paradise—gesturing with her hands—some kind of incoherent sign language I'd never figure out. But apparently she and Levi were on the same page.

"Paisley." Levi blocked my view. He leaned across the drums and whispered, "She's his sister."

My blood pressure plunged.

THUMP

       Thump

            thump.

I was an idiot.

And the crowd did matter.

"Oh God," I squeaked. "Please don't move an inch."

Levi hid me behind his thick frame. I had no idea what to do next. Suddenly, the little drum stool felt like a pedestal. I'd just put it all out there all right, my whole jealous fit for everyone to see.

But I hadn't just embarrassed myself. We were onstage in a honky-tonk with a gathering group of regulars and a few invited guests.

Waylon stomped around Levi. Cal and Paradise flanked him. I was surrounded.

Waylon flicked the pick on his thumb as if he were trying to spark a flame from a cigarette lighter. "Paisley." He sounded out of gas, desperate. "We've been friends a long time. I, I always thought I could count on you. But now." He stopped flicking. He glanced at Paradise, then drew a bead on me. "What do you want, Paisley? 'Cause if it's not the band . . . I mean, what do you really want?"

The band stood in front of me with their dreams on the line. Cal's hands squeezed around the neck of his guitar. His homemade dagger tattoo carved onto his thumb pointed at me. Paradise clutched his accordion to his chest, waiting to hear my answer. No point now in trying to hide that I might have feelings for him. I wouldn't be able to dodge that anymore. Furthermore, they all knew. Even if they didn't, they suspected.

The chatter around the dance floor grew louder as the dinner crowd moved from the taco bar into the cantina. They wouldn't sit idle for long and wait on us to get our act together. Soon they'd start dropping quarters in the jukebox. We'd be done before we ever got going.

I picked up my sticks, ripe to count us in. The dream to be a drummer had never changed for me. It just wasn't the only desire anymore, and I was tired of tucking my dreams and feelings away.

I'd had enough of that. Enough of holding my feelings in my heart. L. V. always said if you keep doin' what you're doin', you'll get more of what you've got. Time to change the results.

Paradise watched me roll the sticks between my fingers. He seemed to figure out what I wanted too. He lifted the cross on his necklace to his lips and kissed it. He turned around, going for his spot behind the center microphone.

I kicked the bass drum then hit the snare—bass-snare, bass-snare—mimicking the natural swing of his backside. Paradise glanced back at me and cocked a grin.

I set the pace, the pace we practiced. "I want it all, Waylon." The other boys backed away from the drums. Cal swung his guitar around, dipped his shoulder, then leaned back and flared up an ear-scorching intro.

I wanted it all.

21

ALONE IN A
CROWDED BAR

A few of what I surmised were cantina regulars spun around the dance floor as we transitioned, like a steady rolling locomotive, from one song to the next. My drumsticks tumbled over the toms, pinged the hi-hat and crash. The vibration from the bass drum shimmied through my body. And since, other than Lacey, I had no one to share in the moment, I drummed for regulars and the band, loving the fact that a beat I drove moved people to get up and dance.

Looking out into the dark bar, I saw Lacey's face glowing in the red neon of the Bud Light sign when Levi went to work on his bass. She came for him. She'd probably heard enough of my banging around the house. Everyone around her went nuts as Levi flipped his baseball cap backward, then dropped the bass tone to a grooving boogie-woogie. The entire Tucker gang had showed up in full force. They were loud and proud.

Cal had his own following. Five of his skateboard buds huddled near a corner table just off the stage. One dude played air guitar right along with Cal. I bet the regulars wondered what the emo kids were doing in a honky-tonk.

Estella clapped her hands over her head as her grandfather, the accordion king, sat beside her, his chest swelling with pride as Paradise sang lead.

Even some of the Sliders showed up, although Waylon's dad stood at the back watching every move with his owl eyes. We were, after all, a Slider band. But he'd have to work hard to nitpick. Waylon had been right about playing like we practiced, and no one lacked focus about what we were doing—especially Waylon. He couldn't have sounded better and his fingers singed his guitar strings and danced up the frets. Even Paradise's grandfather shifted his gaze for a brief moment to take in Waylon's gift.

We closed out a song. Levi kept the beat going while I rested my sticks and positioned the *caja*. Rub and stroke, rub and stroke. It was Paradise's turn. When he drew out the bellows on his accordion, folks began to whoop and holler. With his body swaying and his head rocking, Paradise squeezed out a little spice to complement the country-rock groove. The dancing couples pushed out of a two-step and pulled into a hip-grinding Latin swing. Some bands might have a fiddle or maybe even a harmonica, but the Waylon Slider Band rocked the accordion. And the accordion worked like gravy on biscuits.

Waylon's father gestured an approving nod from the back of the room, and I thought Waylon would levitate. The family pride in the room was wall busting.

A bead of sweat trickled down my back as I put the *caja* down and returned to my drumsticks. I bowled a fifteen-stroke roll across the drumheads, barely holding the sticks as they bounced in my hand. I tossed one stick, catching it in midair as it somersaulted over my head. Never. Missed. A. Beat.

I checked to make sure Lacey saw it. Her eyes were locked on Levi.

Among the crowd and the guitars and the accordion and the dancers, I had never felt so alone.

I wanted my dad to hear me play, watch every stick spinning, bass kick, and roll. I wanted to see him circle his finger in the air like he does when his young pitchers nail their first curveball. "That's it," he'd say. "Bring that every time." I wanted to look out and see L. V. leaning against the bar, telling everyone his niece was the drummer. And I wanted my mother there—complaining about Waylon and how this was all beneath her. But I wanted her there. If for no other reason than to show her that I could do this. Forever, it seemed, all I ever wanted was to play drums. That wasn't enough anymore. Now I wanted to play drums for somebody. And somebody included my family. Without them, drumming felt as hollow as a blown bottle rocket. Nothing left after the big boom except a sour, burning smell lingering in the air.

I closed my eyes, feeling the ricochet of each beat. My arms never tired. My hands never cramped. The drumbeats circled above me, around me like machine-gun fire, like I was down in some foxhole, all the action taking place above.

Then it was over.

And when it's over, it's really over. Nothing left but me and the sticks.

The voices and clapping drew closer to the stage. Cal's friends swarmed him. I tried to ignore the whoops of happy Tuckers as I sat behind my drums like a kid in a playpen.

Finally, Lacey made her way to me. Watching her glide toward me with a smile as bright as a summer afternoon lifted my spirits.

Then she tossed her keys over the drums to me. "We're all going to hang out by Moon Lake." She glanced back at Levi. The smile was all his. "Oh, and park my car on the back side of the Tucker Barn then just walk down. You'll see everyone."

Lacey left the cantina with Levi and the rest of the band. The jukebox kicked on. Couples glided across the dance floor. The neon Bud Light sign above the bar blinked on and off and on and off like a no-vacancy marquee at a cheap, roadside motel. I was the last one to leave the stage. Not that anyone noticed. Not that anyone cared.

22

ASSUMPTIONS

Moon Lake wasn't really a lake at all. It was a crescent-shaped slough carved into the wooded bottom of the Tuckers' land. From tip end to tip end, Moon Lake stretched across the Jessup and Prosper county borders. And on cold, clear spring nights when the dark water soaked up the real moonlight, the old slough looked as if a sliver of the moon had come to rest on earth.

I hid Lacey's car on the back side of the barn and walked toward the hillside where everyone had gathered. I set out, trying to step around the pillowy patches of wildflowers. Not sure what I'd find at the campfire on the hill.

An unnatural light cut into the pasture, blinding me in the moment. The light dimmed and Paradise eased beside me, the hard top off his Bronco. He stopped.

"Thanks." I rubbed my eyes. "Now I know how deer feel."

Paradise opened his passenger door. "Get in before someone runs you over."

I stepped in, moving a brown paper bag on the seat.

"Careful with that," he said. "Don't open it. Had to pick up a few things on my way out here."

"What is it?" I started to unroll the top of the sack despite his demand. "Beer? Cigarettes?"

He shook his head like I offended him, twisted his hand around the steering wheel. "So that's what you assume, what you expect from me?"

I said nothing and started to open the sack.

Paradise hit the brakes, reached his hand across, smashed the sack closed. "It's weed." His hat shaded his face from the moonlight, but I could see his eyes focus on my ring. "And condoms. Stuff you don't need to be around."

I let go of the sack. "Nice." Mother's rant about bands and pot smokers clanged in my head. "Remind me to wear a hazmat suit the next time you give me a ride."

"Your face is red, Paisley." He shifted the Bronco into reverse and backed between the other trucks up to the campfire. "What will they all think?"

I couldn't have cared less what everyone thought. I did, however, care that he seemed to plan on drugs and sex as part of the post-gig after-party. Furthermore, I had to tell Waylon. The band couldn't afford to let Paradise loose in Austin. I hopped out of the Bronco. Lacey and I were leaving whether she wanted to or not.

In the campfire light, Cal and some of his friends huddled in a small circle despite the fact that lawn chairs sat empty around the fire. I was sure I saw the hot end of a cigarette glow. Levi made use of at least one chair, and he held Lacey in his lap—both of them cozied up under a blanket.

Paradise dropped the tailgate on the Bronco and opened the sack.

"You bring something for me too?" Levi's hands were hid under the blanket. All that talk about how he didn't want to let Dad down was just crap.

"Lacey." I almost panicked. "I, we need to go."

"Paisley." Paradise reached into the sack. He pulled out a box of chocolate bars, a bag of marshmallows, and some graham crackers. He pitched the marshmallows at me. "You gonna help?"

Lacey leaned back on Levi's chest. She eyeballed my hand squeezing the bag of marshmallows. "Relax, sis. I texted Mother. She's not looking for us until after midnight." Lacey nodded at Waylon, who sat on the tailgate of his truck fingering his six-string. "And no one here bites."

"Don't tell her that." Paradise pressed his thumbs along the bent corners of a metal coat hanger, straightening it into a skewer.

Lacey giggled. Waylon strummed louder.

I split the top of the marshmallow bag and laid it on his tailgate next to the chocolate bars. Paradise stood by the fire, carefully searing the end of the hanger until all the plastic coating was gone and it was safe to melt the marshmallows.

The night air chilled me to the bone. I rubbed the tops of my arms to warm them and moved closer to the flames. The fire popped and spit bits of neon orange sparks into the dark night.

I probably needed to apologize for assuming the worst in him.

"S'mores?" I asked him, watching the flames dance around the logs.

"Who said the sack was empty?"

He'd tricked me once but not again. "If you think I'm going to double-check, you're wrong."

Paradise held the hanger, cooling it until he could pinch the red-hot tip between his forefingers. He grabbed a marshmallow and stuffed it on the end. "Hold this in the fire." He kept his hand on mine and moved behind me, reaching around my ribs, gently clutching me to him.

I took a deep breath and my heart skipped like a rock on a pond.

"Hey, Waylon," Paradise called out. I felt his breath move through my hair like a warm whisper. "What's that song? Something about the Texas moon?"

Waylon strummed a few chords on his guitar.

"How does it go?" Paradise hummed some until Waylon piped in a few words.

Levi and Lacey quit talking.

Cal peeked around the fire, watching and listening.

Waylon sang in as natural a voice as he spoke. No gooselike nasal honk. No wheezy breathing. Paradise had gotten him to sing without Waylon ever thinking about it. And it wasn't half bad. Kind of twangy, but honest and authentic sounding. We'd all assumed Waylon couldn't sing, but he could. He just needed for someone to believe in him and Paradise did.

Waylon continued to play his guitar and sing in the cold night. I pulled the skewer from the fire. The marshmallow smoked some, but the outside was a dark honey color. Paradise squeezed it and a square of chocolate between two graham crackers.

I took the top cracker off and pulled my finger through the gooey middle. I closed my eyes and sucked all the chocolaty, marshmallowy goodness off my fingertip. When I opened my eyes, Paradise was watching. I licked off the last bit of chocolate.

Paradise cleaned off his tailgate and slammed it shut.

"You know," I began to explain my theory on assumptions. "Someone drowned in Moon Lake once. Mistook it for a real lake. He was wading along the water's edge when he stepped into a hole and went under. He tried to swim out. But he drowned in three feet of water when all he had to do was stand up."

Paradise slipped his hand into his pocket and pulled out his keys. He opened the passenger door. "Get in, Paisley."

23

COWBOY, TAKE ME AWAY

Paradise parked on the edge of Moon Lake and spread a blanket in the back of the Bronco. The water shined like sterling and lay still, undisturbed by Waylon's voice and his six-string drifting down from the hill. The more he pushed his vocals, the stronger his voice became. I could almost hear Waylon begin to believe in himself.

The bluebonnets flung across the pasture under the starlit night reminded me of a patchwork quilt pieced together in swatches of purple, indigo, and evergreen. I sat on the tailgate with my knees tucked against my chest. Paradise lay beside me. His long legs hanging off the tailgate. His hat resting on his chest.

"So where does an accordion prince go when he graduates from the grandfather-tutor-home-travel school?" I asked, feeling the pressure of his finger rubbing along my belt.

"I took the same SATs as everyone else. I can go most anywhere. But I'm enrolled at the University of Geneva in Switzerland for next year. It's where my mother went."

"Sounds fancy." I got that awkward, less-than feeling that always happens when kids at school talk about their summer beach trips and I throw out that we went to Galveston. "And far away. And cold."

"All of the above," he said. "But it's a step for me. I want to be a Rhodes scholar."

I watched his cowboy hat rise and fall with his every breath. He wasn't fitting my idea of scholar. "Weren't presidents Rhodes scholars?"

Paradise patted my hip. "And Kris Kristofferson."

The cool breeze in the night carried Waylon's voice. "I can't believe you got Waylon to sing."

Paradise kept his eyes on the stars. "Waylon needs to quit worrying about what his family thinks. Do his thing. Go wide-open." He hooked a finger in my belt loop and tugged me closer to him. "Like somebody else I know."

Coyotes howled in the distance. I squeezed my arms around my shins, hugging my knees tight to my chest. He had the ability to move me with a single finger. I didn't trust myself to be that close, to touch him.

I picked at the toe of my boot, trying not to look at him stretched out in the moonlight. "Since when do you care about Waylon Slider?"

"Hate seeing somebody want something and letting fear or embarrassment or circumstances hold them back. I play accordion, Paisley. And I'm bringing it back to cool." Paradise pulled my belt loop again, inching me closer to him. He rubbed his hand across my back, lifting my shirttail. His middle finger traced the curve of my spine.

It was as if a covey of quail had burst into flight inside my chest. "Aren't you"—I stuttered—"aren't you afraid Waylon will drop you now that he's singing?"

Paradise laughed, tossed his hat into the front seat. "Too close to Texapalooza to drop this boy. Besides"—he pulled me on top of him, slipping his hand into my back pocket—"his drummer would kick his ass."

In his arms, I slowly unfolded like a love note read in secret. My face pressed against his chest. I held on to him and the feeling of being wanted. Not alone like I was at the cantina. From his black T-shirt to the hard muscle running across his shoulder up his neck to the soft curl just behind his ear, Paradise smelled and tasted like the sweet, smoky mesquite burning on the campfire.

I gave up fighting the pull to touch him and was no longer sure why I fought it in the first place. Nothing about this felt wrong.

He peeled off his shirt. I felt it slip from above my arms. Felt the smooth warmth of his bare chest.

The stars above us shined down like spotlights. Waylon's singing stopped and Lacey's laughter cut through the night air. The graduation picture of Mother in her cap with the black gown covering her swollen belly like a tent crept into my mind. I had the urge, the sudden need to put both feet on the ground. Grab hold of the momentum. Think it all through.

I pushed him away, scooted to the tailgate's edge, and stood up. The grass was almost knee-high and I prayed it was still too cool for snakes.

"Let me guess." Paradise sat on the tailgate. He picked at a hole in the knee of his jeans. "This has something to do with that one-life-one-love-ring thing."

His legs were slightly open. Open enough for me to slip between them. I ran my index finger down the sternum of his bare chest, stopping at the button on his jeans. "This has to do with me needing to slow down. Catch my breath."

Paradise clasped his hands around my hips. His thumbs touching just below my belly button. His breath warm on my neck. His lips tickled my ear. "Have you caught it?"

My pulse quickened like it does when I'm drumming in a hard rock groove, a furious push to a quick end. I brushed my fingers through his hair. "It's probably close to time for Lacey and me to head home."

He kissed me, then whispered, "Paisley, I love that you're fearless. You know what you want. Don't let some fake, forced promise scare you." His hands pressed around me. "This is between you and me. Don't be afraid to say yes."

"I'm not afraid to say yes to you." A part of me wanted to. I held on to him. "But I'm also not afraid to say no."

Paradise dropped his hands from my hips as if I'd vanished, as if he never had hold in the first place. "Fine then." Paradise shoved the blanket into a wad and slammed the tailgate.

I watched him put his shirt back on, punching his arms through the sleeves. "I'd rather you not be mad," I said.

Paradise stomped around the Bronco. A low-hanging tree branch swayed in front of him. "Hummph." He grunted like a rutting buck and struck the limb with a fierce slap. The leaves quivered; the limb snapped.

"I'll walk back up the hill." I set out for the campfire.

"Wait." He put his hat on and opened the passenger door. "I drove you down here; I'll drive you back."

"No thanks." I slipped around him. "You're mad and picking fights with trees. Think I'll pass on the ride."

"Fine," Paradise warned. "Move quickly in case of water moccasins."

I stood knee-deep in the tall grass. "It's dark. How am I supposed to watch for snakes?"

He ignored me and cranked the Bronco. The passenger door was still open. I jumped for the seat. "This is not me giving in," I said as I slammed the door.

Paradise shifted into low gear then rested his hand on my leg, his fingers pressing against my thigh. "This is not me giving up."

WHEN THE SMOKE CLEARS

I'm stuck throwing rocks at this campfire tonight
Watching the sparks fly and the embers smolder
You're down the hill with him
I should be stronger and put up a fight
I guess I failed to mention
I've been trying to get your attention.

Throwing rocks at the flame
I can't compete with his game
He's all hard muscle and heartbreak and swagger
Yeah, I'm not much of a threat with just a skateboard
   and ink dagger.
But when the smoke clears
I'll still be here.

I've been on the outskirts all my life
The edge of this fire ain't nothing new
So I don't have the ride or the hat or the boots
Those things don't make me less of a man
They don't make me feel less than
It's only your indifference that can.

He's your white hot flame
Styled hair, exotic name
Me, I'm just a slow burning ember
He may forget your face, but I'll always remember
And when the fire dies down
Look around
The smoke will clear
And you'll find me here.

24

JUICY DETAILS

Lacey parked me in front of the tri-fold salon mirror in her bedroom. Her hair swept into a business-like ponytail. Her makeup kit fanned open with tray after tray of blushes, eye shadows, and lipsticks. A makeup-brush apron tied in a firm knot at her waist. She wasn't just passing a Sunday afternoon getting my face "stage ready" as she called it. Lacey had another agenda.

"Juicy details," she said as she dabbed concealer under my eyes. "Out with them."

I stared in the mirror, watched the shades in my face even out to a single mannequin-like beige. "I hate to disappoint you," I said. "But nothing really happened last night."

"Liar." Lacey blew into a brush. Puffs of powder clouded the air. "Something always happens. So, you kissed him. Start there."

I twisted in the chair. The stupid salon cape choked my neck. My puttied-up face itched like it had a sticky coating of honey. "Nothing happened," I repeated. "And why do you think I need to wear so much makeup at Texapalooza?"

"Stage lights wash everybody out. You'll thank me when you see pictures."

Pictures! Like I'd have anyone there to take pictures. The guys were all bringing family and friends. I'd spent a lot of time and effort sneaking around to get there, but now it started to bug me that I had no family to play for.

Lacey spun a slim brush around on a red lipstick tip. "Sweet Cherry Pie. Perfect." She painted the color on my lips. "So you kissed him, and then?"

I must've looked like I'd sucked a lemon.

"Oh God," she said. "Does he dip?"

"NO!" I yelled it loud enough that Mother and Dad could've probably heard it down by the barn. "Lacey, he doesn't dip. He wasn't drinking. He didn't throw me to the ground and pounce on me like some rabid dog."

"Really?" Lacey raised her eyebrows as she sharpened an eye pencil. "I find that hard to believe." She twisted the eyebrow pencil until the scraping yielded a fine point. "So, at what body part did the touching stop?"

I closed my eyes and let her draw over the lid. In my mind, I could see Paradise's bare shoulders and feel how my nose tickled when it brushed his earring. "I don't know," I told her. "But when I needed to slow down, he did."

"Hmmph." Lacey's hand pressed against my forehead and her brushing intensified the more I talked.

"He never tried to force me to do anything," I said.

Lacey stopped. I felt her hands ease off my face. "Well, that's a new one." She fumbled around in her makeup kit like she was looking for something she misplaced. "Certainly not my luck."

My sister had long since broken the promise we made to Mother and Dad. I wasn't sure when exactly it happened for her or who the guy was. But I knew. And now my promise reminder, my silver pu-rity ring, seemed to squeeze tight around my finger. I had made a promise I didn't fully understand when the thought of being with a boy in that way was just plain gross and something I'd never do. No one ever warned me that I'd actually want to. Now my mind was stuck with a promise my body wanted to break. "How do you know when you're ready?" I unsnapped the salon cape. "I mean for, you know, that?"

The blue in her eyes turned as dark and hard as cobalt. "If you have to ask, then just keep saying no." Lacey tightened her ponytail, picked up the eyeliner, and started on my other eye. "I like doing hair and makeup, Paisley. If I don't like it, I change it. If I mess it up, I fix it. Lip color and hairstyles aren't forever. Sex is. You don't get a do-over once you start. You never get that first time back."

"Feels right," I said. "I like being with him, and I think it runs both ways."

"God, Paisley. I'm sure you do. I guarantee he does. They all do." Lacey leaned against the dresser. "Have you ever eaten a whole bowl of cookie dough?" Lacey shaped her hands into a circle about the size of Mother's mixing bowl.

I had not, but I got the feeling Lacey had.

"It's all there for the taking. It looks good. It tastes good. And in the moment, it feels good. Later, not so much." She straightened my bangs with her fingertips. "Back slowly away from the cookie dough, Paisley. Time changes things. I'm going to tell you something Mother can't or won't tell you because it'd make her out to be a big ol' hypo-crite. Don't be afraid to give yourself some time. Keep that boy at arm's length. He's not going anywhere."

The corners of her lips turned down when she smiled.

"And don't make that decision in a truck by the lake. You've got to make the choice before you get all drunk on hard muscles and soft lips."

"What about Levi?" I asked her. "Juicy details. Out with them."

She gently swept eye shadow in long strokes across my lids. "Levi's a gentleman," she said. "But he's going to go off God-knows-where to school, and I'm going to stay here and go to beauty college. I'm focusing on me and he's OK with that."

"Lacey." I watched her in the mirror as she hunted for another eye shadow. "Do you ever think about getting out of Prosper County?"

"One town's just as good as the next." She took a thin brush and painted the crease of my eyelid. "Mother thinks Prosper County is the armpit of the state, but that's only because she was too beat down to leave. I'm betting folks around here, especially the Big Wells Country Club crowd, treated her like she was a low-class county kid who got knocked up by the major leaguer on purpose. After a while, I'm guessing she quit fighting and just started believing whatever they said and took her place on the bottom rung of the social ladder."

Lacey might've been right. Mother might've quit fighting for herself, but that changed when we came along. Mother placed a high value on making sure no one looked down their nose at us.

Lacey popped her gum. "I don't think Mother ever owned her roots—not her hair roots—you know, her country roots. I think the thought of her stepping outside the county and having people ask her where she left her horse pushed the limits of her pride." Lacey brushed the corner of my eye with her ring finger. "I ain't running from nothing, certainly not who I am or where I'm from. I'm running to something, Paisley, and so are you." Lacey laughed. "If someone wants to know where I left my horse, I'll tell 'em I hitched it to my oil well."

"You don't have an oil well."

"I don't have a horse either." Lacey lifted the bottom tray from her makeup kit. "You really want the juicy, juicy details?" She handed me an envelope addressed to Glamour Beauty College, Financial Aid Department. "Mailing that off tomorrow. Mother can refuse to pay or say we don't have the money. It won't matter. I qualify."

Her slow, methodical march around Mother to get into beauty school, to leave the singing behind, was starting to look like a well-executed battle won. "You're really doing this?"

"Yep." Lacey had a little gleam in her eye. "And here's the real kicker. Last week when I was trimming Uncle L. V.'s hair, he asked me why I wasn't going to school to get a cosmetology license."

I smiled. I could just hear him saying, "Do the thing you love to do. Hank Williams died at the ripe old age of twenty-nine. Stevie Ray Vaughan at thirty-five. Jesus at thirty-three. Don't think you're special and the Lord's gonna bless you with time."

"Paisley, he told me he'd pay for beauty school if I'd promise to follow that by getting a college degree in business or marketing. So I'd know how to manage a salon."

"He's right," I told her. "You should do that."

Lacey held a fat tube of mascara. "This whole Texapalooza thing got me to thinking. You're making your dreams come true. I know what I want to do, so I'm making it happen for me." Then she added, "You and I just have different ways of doing business."

"You've got to tell Mother," I reminded her. The thought certainly nagged at me often enough.

Lacey slammed the mascara down. "After the fit she pulled when Dad told her about Levi, I don't feel the need to share anything with her. She can find out when everybody else does. And she can like it or not."

Lacey whisked an unnatural blush—sparkly pink—over my cheeks. Maybe the take-it-or-leave-it approach could work for her. Probably would. But not for me. I had two years of high school left under the Tillery roof, and one more thing I'd come to realize. I actually cared what Mother thought. I didn't need her approval, but I wanted her acceptance and maybe even her presence. For me the dream wasn't just to get out of Prosper County and drum anymore, it was to play it out—flams, rim shots, rolls. I wanted my family, all of them, to be a part.

"Look at the ceiling." Lacey took the mascara and painted my eyelashes. "Beautiful. The smoky eye is perfect. Damn, I'm good." She stepped back, admiring her work. "We're going to not only get you to Austin next week. You're going to be the hottest drummer in town."

I looked in the mirror. "Not exactly Happy the Clown." The color on my eyes wasn't bad. "The red lipstick has to go, though. Maybe tone down the blush too."

Lacey smiled at me in her bittersweet way. "Levi said the guys are leaving early next Saturday."

I nodded.

"How are you getting to Austin?" she asked.

"I'm going with the band." That was the first time I'd said it, and the first time it seemed real. "I'll tell them this week to pick me up early, before dawn at the bridge down from L. V.'s."

Lacey shook her head. "That's running away. Even I wouldn't try that."

"I can if you cover for me. It's just for a little more than twenty-four hours. If they start asking questions, just tell them the truth. Austin is six hours away. By the time they figure it out, we'll have already performed."

"I have to cover for you my way." Lacey took a deep breath. "Here's the real juicy detail. I've already told Mother that you and I are going with a friend to her church's youth retreat early Saturday. We won't be back until late Sunday." Lacey put her hands together like an innocent praying angel. She squealed, "I'm going to Austin with you."

I sat numb, processing every single word she said—especially the part where she said she was going to Austin. I threw her salon cape on the floor. "You're not going with me. You're going with Levi." The mascara burned when my eyes began to tear. "This is the most important thing ever for me, and you've gone and screwed it up." I wanted to slap her. I couldn't believe she'd be that selfish.

"I've done this for you, Paisley. Is Levi's family going? Yes. Do I want to see him play? Yes. But I'm taking you there, not him. This way you're not running away. You're with me." Lacey picked the cape off the floor. "Everyone else in that band will have family there. If I don't go, you'll have no one."

Lacey knew me better than I thought. I dabbed my eyes with a tissue. I was almost sure she was sincere.

"You've gone and messed up my artwork." She took the tissue away from me and patted more concealer under my eyes.

I ran down a mental checklist of the details of her plan: Mother would expect us to leave early. The youth retreat gave us a reason to be gone all weekend. No running away.

"I'm going to do your makeup," she said. "And I'm bringing my camera."

She sounded like Mother.

"A youth retreat?" I rolled my eyes. "Really, Lacey." But the more I thought about it, the more I thought Lacey's plan might actually work. Regardless, we were a week away from taking the stage at Texapalooza. I had no choice but to stick with her plan and focus on my drumming. Getting to Austin was just one part. Being good enough to stand out was the other. My adrenaline whirled inside me like a rapid roll on a snare drum. Everything had come down to this. The band was really taking the show to Austin. Other than Mother, nothing could get in the way. But I misjudged my own sister.

25

INCENTIVES

On my way to rehearsal on Monday, I passed Uncle L. V. chugging across the pasture in his big green John Deere. The shredder buzzed low over the ground—a clear sign he was manicuring his ryegrass runway.

I stopped the four-wheeler and waved to him. No use. From the looks of the high grass edging a narrow, short strip, L. V. was just getting started. He maintained his runway as well as he did his planes' engines. He'd keep an intense focus on his mowing and probably stay on the tractor until close to dark, until the grass runway was as tidy and perfect as a country club fairway.

I loved riding with him when I was younger—the constant buzz in the seat, the *chugga-chugga* bounce, the jolt of an unexpected *thwunk* into a hole.

I hit the throttle on the four-wheeler, shooting straight for the hangar. Everything laid out. A perfect plan. My drums. The band. The thrill of playing in Austin at Texapalooza in front of me.

And Paradise. He leaned against the outside of the hangar in the spotlight of the April sun.

"Wow." I turned the engine off and swung my right leg over the handlebars, sitting sideways on the seat. I counted the trucks. "The closer we get to the contest this weekend, the earlier you all seem to want to get going."

"Can't start without you." Paradise glanced across the pasture. L. V., a distant hum. Paradise leaned down, his hat casting a shadow across my face. The sun had warmed his chest, and I wasn't sure if he'd pulled me to him or I'd gravitated there on my own. His lips were as soft as the flannel of his shirt.

A chain swinging from the flagpole in front of L. V.'s house clanged with every steady breath of wind. A dull *tink-tink, tink-tink*.

"I guess this means you're over being mad," I said.

He held me tighter, so I took the hug as a yes. I could've stayed cuddled in his arms. But this was the last week we had to practice. Not even the dizzying possibility of being wrapped up in Paradise could fog my vision of Texapalooza. I wasn't about to let anyone or anything slow us, the band, down.

I let go of Paradise and pulled my sticks from my back pocket. We had a summer ahead of us to spend with each other, but less than a week to be perfect in Austin. "Get moving." I drummed on his chest. "We can't risk sloppy squeezebox playing."

Paradise stared at me long enough for me to weigh a warning in his eyes. "Speaking of risk." He held up a set of keys. Keys with a plump silver heart chain. Lacey's keys. "Your sister's been here. Awhile." He jabbed the toe of his boot at a tire on the four-wheeler. "I saw her car from the road before I ever crossed the cattle guard. Thought I'd better move it before someone else sees it."

I gripped my sticks in my fist.

Paradise grabbed my upper arm, squeezing as I bolted for the hangar. "Easy," he said. "Levi was as surprised as the rest of us."

"Don't worry about moving the car." I snatched the keys from his hand. "She's leaving."

Inside the hangar, Lacey sat sideways in a lawn chair with her legs draped over one arm. The place reeked of nail polish. Waylon must've broken a string because his guitar lay on its back while he worked with the intensity of a surgeon. Cal sat cross-legged on the floor with his journal across his lap. Levi stood helpless with his hands on hips and his bass guitar hanging around his neck like a coach's whistle.

I dropped Lacey's keys in her lap. "Leave."

"Chill out, Paisley." She twisted the cap on a bottle of pink polish. "I'm just watching."

"You're not just watching. You're stealing time with Levi." I gritted my teeth. "The band's time."

Waylon and his labored breathing huffed beside me. No one wanted her here. Lacey was a weed in the garden.

"There are lots of reasons why you are leaving. None of which I'm covering now." I was embarrassed for her. Embarrassed for me. "Just go. We don't have time for distractions."

Lacey spun around in the chair. "Then maybe you should get yourself to drumming and not make a scene." She crossed her legs and wiggled the toes on her right foot so that her flip-flop slapped against her heel.

Waylon threw up his hands. "If your mother sees your car and gets curious, then you've killed this for us." He sucked in a deep breath that shook his entire body. "W-w-wiped out everything we've worked for. No Texapalooza. No band. No drummer." Waylon was losing his grip on whatever confidence he'd gained at the campfire.

Lacey kept swinging her foot and popping her flip-flop. *Wap. Wap. Wap.* More concerned about drying her toenail polish than Waylon's drama. She knew him too well to be moved by his dismal prediction.

Getting Lacey to leave would take more than trying to lay a guilt trip on her. This was after all my sister who never even tried to stop or slow down when innocent squirrels darted in front of her car. The best consolation after the thud was a "whooopsee" and a giggle. Sympathizing with others wasn't her strong suit. Lacey needed incentive.

I leaned over Lacey where only she could hear me.

"With one word from me, you don't go to Austin. The rest will say you can't go. Levi will tell you to stay home."

Lacey blinked and looked away.

"You can leave now and we'll go as planned."

The hum from L. V.'s tractor buzzed the hangar as he rounded back down the runway. "If you don't leave on your own, I'll get Uncle L. V. to move you."

Lacey knew Uncle L. V. had zero patience for drama. She stood up, grabbed her giant purse, and mumbled something that sounded like *pissy.*

Paradise chuckled as he rolled his shoulders under the accordion straps.

Levi tried to say good-bye to Lacey at the doorway to the hangar.

She slipped between him and his guitar. Lacey kissed him. And kissed him. For a long time she just dangled from his lips like a ripe peach about to drop in L. V.'s orchard.

Performance kissing was Lacey's style, not mine. I wanted to crawl under the tarp covering my drums until she finally had both feet on the ground and disappeared from the hangar.

"Think what y'all want to"—Levi stretched his guitar strap over his shoulder—"but that was worth it."

"Unless my mother shows up." I gathered the tarp. Before I could lay it to the side, I noticed Waylon sitting in a chair with his hands cupped over his face. I wasn't sure if he was hyperventilating or praying. "You all right, Waylon?"

Waylon rubbed his face. He reached into a backpack sprawled at his feet and pulled out a few sheets of paper, handing us each one. The top of the page read, ITINERARY.

"It's our final schedule for Texapalooza," he said. "They had some bands drop out so they're starting later. They changed our time."

Paradise threw his fist in the air. "We're at night now."

Levi picked a couple bass strings and sang, "Primetime."

Cal and I watched as Paradise and Levi performed some shoulder-bumping man ritual. Waylon sank back into the chair.

I sorted through it all. Night meant a much bigger crowd, bright stadium lights, a big stage in one of the biggest music towns in the country. This was the dream. I was up for it. I even thought about shoulder bumping Cal. Unfortunately, I took one look at Waylon with his head buried in his hands and my throat began to ache. Choke.

"Waylon, c'mon." I squatted beside him. "This is the best thing that could've happened."

Waylon shoved an itinerary at me. He pointed at our time slot. "What does that say?"

"Nothing." I didn't see anything wrong. "'Six o'clock, The Waylon Slider Band.'"

He shook his head. "Nothing. Nothing?" Waylon stood up and kicked the tarp mounded on the floor by my drums. "If we blow this, I'll be the biggest embarrassment my family's ever known. My dad told me not to use my name, but I did it anyway. And he told me I wasn't ready for this and he was right."

"Maybe you're not ready." Paradise half ignored Waylon and started riffing on his accordion. "But the rest of us are. Man up. Get on your guitar."

"Don't be so rude," I snapped, feeling like I was trying to hold water in a sieve.

Paradise pounded the heel of his boot against the concrete. "I could use a beat here."

I didn't budge. I couldn't believe Paradise would just ignore Waylon like that. But then Cal started playing, and Levi. It was like I was the only one concerned about Waylon. However, whatever methods the guys were using delivered. Waylon got his guitar and went hard at the chords.

I hustled back to my drums. We'd lost too much rehearsal time already. But if Waylon was playing, I was too. Paradise stepped behind the drums and whispered in my ear, "Let him work it out on his guitar. Just keep drumming."

I settled down. Playing was the one thing I could handle. Control what I could control and feel the clock start to tick on Texapalooza.

26

CATCHING WIND

By Thursday afternoon, we were just forty-eight hours shy of taking the stage at Texapalooza. It was one of those intense spring days when green pine tops and full leafy peach trees and pure white clouds contrast with the blue sky, surreal in the bright sunlight.

The hangar doors pulled the full width open. The guys stood outside watching Uncle L. V. race *Miss Molly Moonlight* down the grass runway, catch the wind under her belly, and rise off the ground—her engines roaring into the blue sky.

None of us said a word, but we all sensed it. A sweet reality that, like *Miss Molly*, we were reaching out and up and grabbing for our own dreams far and away from Prosper County.

Paradise pressed his hand against his stomach.

I jabbed him with a drumstick. "If you take a deep breath right as the wheels leave the ground, you won't lose your lunch."

"Get serious, Paisley." Waylon had his skull cap on as if this practice were a dress rehearsal. "Somebody get the doors."

"Oh, leave them open." I looked out at the acres of rolling pasture and deep green thickets, and pointed a drumstick outside.

"Imagine a whole bunch of folks waiting to hear the Waylon Slider Band."

Waylon's face went tomato red. He still wasn't comfortable with the notion of a bigger spotlight on us.

"And the peach grove to the left"—Levi rolled the brim of his baseball cap between his palms—"that's the groupies."

Even though Levi kidded him, none of us called Waylon on his self-doubt. Not even me. I was beginning to understand their guy-talk better. Playing out the nerves instead of talking them out. And I trusted Waylon's guitar to give him more confidence than any encouragement I might try to prop him up with. Furthermore, his insecurities were about to be tapped. I had something new to spring on Waylon.

The band waited on me to count them in, but I rested my sticks on the snare. "I'm going to try a different opening," I said, knowing full well that Waylon would blow up over the very idea this close to showtime. Still, I knew deep down he trusted me with the beat. Any opposition would most likely be out of fear, and Waylon was going to need to get past fear if he planned on getting anywhere.

Waylon put his hands on hips and stared at the rafters. "No way, Paisley."

"I'm counting us in with the *caja*." I put the little drum between my legs and drew out the basic one, two, three, four, but with a twist. I added a skip, a saucy *umph* between the hard counts. I repeated it; the rhythm echoed inside the hangar. "C'mon." I steadily drew out an *umpapa-umph*, *umpapa-umph*. "Small drum, big sound. It makes a statement, Waylon. We're not just another copycat country band."

"We can't haul off and throw down a new opening. We don't have enough time to get it right." Waylon fought the idea, but he didn't say he didn't like the sound.

We all trusted Waylon, and it was high time he trusted us. "Leave the percussion to your drummer, Waylon." I knew opening with the *caja* would be sweet, a twist with the groove.

"Lay the count down again." Levi readied his bass guitar.

I did and he linked up at the right time, same as always. Cal lit up the Gibson with his signature riff.

"The *caja*'s like salt." I had Waylon's attention. "Opening with it changes nothing. It just brings out the flavor."

"Dude, what she's sayin' . . ." Levi put his hand on Waylon's shoulder. "Heck, I don't know what she's sayin', but it sounds good. So does that bongo thing." He pointed at the *caja*.

Paradise had been silent, probably afraid if he uttered a word, Waylon would turn on him and say the whole intro change was his idea. He might even refuse to use it just to keep from giving in to Paradise. But Waylon had already given in, he just couldn't see it. Every rehearsal since the bonfire at Moon Lake when Paradise got Waylon to sing, Paradise had been backing off parts of songs. Waylon had continued to sing. The more Paradise backed off, the stronger Waylon's voice held out. Waylon didn't seem to realize it, but Paradise—always more interested in his accordion than singing—was pulling the lead vocals out of him. Paradise was giving Waylon his band.

"What do you want to do, Waylon?" Paradise eased the issue forward. "Give it a run-through?"

Waylon finally trusted me. "Don't dress it up with a bunch of fills in between the count," he said. "Keep it pure. It's a Latin drum. It's going to sound like a Latin drum. You don't need to try to spell that out between the counts."

My heart bounced into my throat. That was as good an approval as Waylon could muster.

Paradise took a step toward me then stopped. I think he would've kissed me if the thought of messing things up hadn't popped in his mind. I settled for a wink.

I counted us in on the *caja*, and we ran through the set we'd play soon for the crowd at Texapalooza—not once, but twice. Song after song. Drumroll after drumroll. Waylon pushing his vocals. Paradise backing off. Cal breathing harmonies like a cooing dove. And Levi plunking bass.

Then Waylon called rehearsal.

"Let's stop before we get bored with our own set." Waylon rarely cut practice short.

I could've played for another hour. Plus, I had that much daylight left and then some.

"I'll help you with the doors, Paisley," Levi said.

Paradise took his hat off, combed his fingers through his hair. "I can handle the doors."

"You good with him handling things?" Levi watched Paradise pack his accordion.

One word from me and Levi would stay.

"He can handle the doors, Levi," I said.

The guys closed up and left one by one. Behind them, Paradise pulled the giant hangar doors shut. The sun was still high enough in the sky to keep the shadows short.

"You got some time?" Paradise clasped his fingers between mine.

"Maybe." We walked around the hangar, stopping by the four-wheeler. I didn't know what he had in mind, but there wasn't anything I was in a hurry to head home for.

I laid my drumsticks across the seat of the four-wheeler. Paradise pulled me toward his Bronco.

"Where are you taking me?" I joked. He wasn't taking me anywhere. I was going on my own.

He opened the passenger door. I climbed in.

"Dancing," he said with a smile.

27

ONE OF THESE NIGHTS

In late spring when the days grow longer, the tall pines shade Moon Lake from the setting sun. And right about twilight, there's a wild whisper of wind that careens through the trees, parts the reeds lining the bank, and sends the lily pads rocking on the water.

Where that wind began, I didn't know. I only knew that it had a life of its own and could sway everything in its path.

I stood at the end of the pier, the toes of my boots slightly beyond the edge. And just to the outside of my boots were those familiar scuffed-up snip-toes. Paradise wrapped his arms around my waist. His belt buckle cold against my lower back. His chin resting on my head. Every now and then after the wind swirled past us, he leaned against me, bending me toward the water, far enough forward that my heels would rise, but not so far as to lose his balance and lose me to the water.

That was where he kept me. On the edge.

An old Eagles song was coming from the Bronco. Paradise turned me around, facing him. My heels hung off the pier. The only thing keeping me out of Moon Lake was the strength of his hand. He kissed my neck and whispered, "I say we go skinny-dipping."

I buried my face in his shirt. Embarrassed and laughing at the same time. "You first."

The Eagles faded, and a two-step beat lapped around us in time with the water against the bank. A rocking country beat. And we danced. Spinning round and round on the pier. Over the water. In the purple haze of twilight. The old quarter-sawn boards creaking with every two-step and twirl.

As the song drifted out and another in, Paradise held me in his arms and pushed his lips against mine in a way that made me forget where I was, forget the time. My feet had long since left the ground. All I could feel and all I could taste was the sweet softness of his lips.

I wanted to stay in that moment, hold tight to it, but Paradise pushed us forward.

He brushed his fingertips along the slope of my neck. His middle finger slipping gently under my bra strap. His hand was hot against my skin and his heart pumped through his palm.

I squeezed his wrist, kissed his hand, and walked away from him to the end of the pier. So much in my life was uncertain. Not just him. The band and school and where I'd end up. Where drumming would take me. I couldn't figure us out, until I figured me out.

Paradise stayed back. I heard him blow out a long, hard breath followed by the clopping of his boots on the pier. He sat down behind me. I pointed at the bright star shining near the moon. "That's Venus."

"How do you know?" Paradise smoothed his hand across my stomach and under my shirt.

"Lots of factors." I leaned back into him. "Starting with it's the clearest, brightest thing in the night sky, *and* it reaches optimum brightness right after the sun sets."

He laughed. His fingertips tickled my ribs. "Did you just say 'optimum brightness'?"

"I'm good in science." I felt compelled to defend my intellect. "And math." I thought about the kids at school who grew up in Big Wells with tutors and social calendars and the purebred, inbred prejudice that rural kids were dumb hicks. I pushed Paradise's hand off my stomach and sat up. "I'm ranked number four in my class. I can quote Mark Twain and the geometry formula for the area of a cone."

The water below us swished as a bass hit a grasshopper. The tree frogs whirred in a mad harmony with the locusts and a lone whip-poor-will.

Paradise fingered a sprig of hair behind my ear. "Whew." His breath danced around my neck. "I'll keep that in mind if I ever need a lecture and a dunce hat."

I swatted his leg. "I'm serious. My grades are important to me." I traced a heart on his leg with my finger. "I may want to be a Rhodes scholar."

Paradise grabbed my head in his hand and kissed me. A long, slow kiss that burned through me and melted my boots. He leaned over, laying my back against the pier. His other hand pushed against my chest.

The weight of him took my breath away. Scared me. If he didn't stop, I wouldn't be strong enough to stop him. I shoved him.

Paradise raised both hands as if I held a gun on him. "A *no* would have been fine."

"I'm not . . I can't . . ." I didn't know what to say, so I just shook my head.

No shouldn't need a discussion, but I went there anyway. "I don't want you to be mad."

"You keep saying that." He twisted the bottom button on my shirt. "Would it change your mind if I said I was?"

"No."

"Then you don't have anything to be sorry for." He kissed my forehead. "I'm all yours." He paused, and I could feel his chest rise with a deep breath. "On your terms."

He hugged me, lifted my feet off the ground, as darkness closed around us. "But if you think you can coax me out here, use me to dance with, then drop me like an old drumstick, you're wrong. I won't be treated like that. I have too much self-respect."

"Coax *you* out here?" We got back in the Bronco. It was dark enough now that he needed the headlights. I'd be way late getting home. Time with Paradise slipped by.

Every time a worry crept into my head, I stared at his hand clasped around mine. Dancing with him on the pier was something I'd never regret regardless. But *regardless* took on a whole new meaning when he pulled up to L. V.'s to let me out. My drumsticks were resting on the handlebars of the four-wheeler. They'd been moved. L. V. wasn't due back until tomorrow. I looked across the thicket. There were only a few people who would've been up here and moved my sticks.

Mother ranked at the top of the list.

28

GHOST NOTES

Musical-themed sugar cookies cut into treble clefs and quarter notes and decorated in black and white covered the kitchen counter. A breeze floated through the screen door and the windows, cooling the kitchen from the heat of the oven and stove.

"You missed dinner." Mother squeezed icing from a fat tube with a tiny pointed tip on the end. Her hands were red and dry from working the cookie dough and ringing the icing bag. She had her hair piled on top of her head in a wonky updo. Definitely not Lacey's work.

"Where's Dad?" I asked. His truck wasn't in the drive.

Mother put the icing bag down. She dabbed her forehead with her sleeve. "It's baseball season, Paisley." She wiped her hands on her apron and smirked. "He's running the batting cages. Probably blowing rays of sunshine up the rear end of every Little League dad who wants to hear his son is the next A-Rod. I'm prepping for a big catering job Saturday. That's what we do. We work." She rubbed her hands as if they ached and rubbing would ease the soreness. "We work so that you girls can have more opportunities than what we had. So you can get an education and get away from here. We don't want you stuck eking out a living in Prosper County."

Mother could've been at L. V.'s. She could've moved my drumsticks. The dig about work came out of the blue.

The screen door opened and Dad stepped in. Mother jumped. She wasn't expecting him.

Dad hung his baseball cap off a cabinet knob and kissed her. "Haven't seen this in a while." Dad pointed at the stitching on her apron. THE KITCHEN GODDESS CATERING. A relic from my elementary-school years and Mother's short-lived attempt at a catering company.

"I'm temporarily back in business." Mother drew in a deep breath. She picked up the icing tube. "I agreed to do a job Saturday."

"Lucky folks," Dad said. "Where have you been?" he asked me. Straight up.

I dodged his question. Not wanting to lie to him. "I just got home."

Dad stared at me. He peeled his leather work gloves off his big hands, and he smelled like fresh-cut grass. Dad had been shredding. He could've moved the sticks. Maybe it was him after all. I thumbed toward Lacey's room. "I'll grab a snack later. Lacey and I need to talk about this weekend."

"Well, don't bother planning on that youth retreat." Mother pulled a fresh batch of music-note cookies from the oven. "Lacey will be trying out for another choir on Saturday. This one from the Bible college over in Jessup County."

"A Bible college?" I could still ride with the guys to Austin. But the very idea of Lacey attending a Bible college sounded like punishment.

No way would she go. She was probably hiding in her room, plotting a very un-Christian maneuver.

Mother carefully slipped a spatula under each note and delicately placed the cookie on parchment paper. "She's in for certain. I've agreed to do some catering jobs for the choir in exchange." Mother gloated over her perfect cookie. "I'll show those Prosper County choir snobs a thing or two."

Mother was a little like Waylon, always trying to prove herself. Somehow, Lacey was wound up in her efforts. I pitched the idea out that maybe her plan was flawed. "I don't think Lacey would be happy going somewhere you had to bribe to get her in."

"Shows you what you know, honey pie." Mother grabbed a wooden rolling pin and pounded flat another batch of cookie dough. "Connections. You scratch my back and I'll scratch yours. Rich people do it all the time." She leaned the force of her weight into the rolling pin. "It's not what you know. It's who you know."

I thought about Waylon and how the Sliders' bluegrass roots ran deep. They knew people who knew people. Waylon relied on none of those connections. Didn't even want them. It was about the music for him. Making a name for himself. Letting his guitar make his introduction.

Dad poured himself a glass of milk. "What do you think about that, Paisley?"

He pushed me to make a stand. So I did. The picture I had of Lacey in Bible college trying to be something she wasn't proved too much to let the charade continue.

"I think it's how hard you work that gets you somewhere. And I think Lacey's done with singing."

"Done? Don't you dare say that to her," Mother gasped. "She needs us to believe in her. Singing is her life's dream." Mother pointed at me with her rolling pin. "You want to talk about hard work. Your father and I work day and night to support you girls. Lacey's gifted. She's going to ride that gift out of Prosper County and we have to believe in her. She's worked year after year to try to make her dreams come true. Hard work."

I watched Mother go off in a cloud of flour.

"From where I stand . . ." I paused and thought about the consequences of what was about to fly out of my mouth. "From where I stand, you're the one doing all the hard work to make sure she gets to sing."

Mother slammed the rolling pin onto the counter. "She doesn't need you running her down with smart-aleck remarks. She needs you supporting her. She's got to pursue her passion or else she'll be stuck in the same old same old." Then Mother added, "Maybe you should get up enough gumption to find your own dream instead of goofing off at L. V.'s every day of the week."

Dad scrubbed his hands and forearms at the sink. He did nothing to come between me and Mother. He wanted me to tell her the truth. I could see it. If ever there was a moment to come clean, this was it. But I was within thirty-two hours of leaving for Austin. Mother would take more work than I had time for. Opportunities didn't always present themselves at the right time. And if it was her who moved my sticks, she'd have said so by now.

If Lacey had to go sing, I still had a ride with the guys. But I feared what she might do and not because of the singing farce. Without knowing it, Mother was separating Lacey from me. She wouldn't be able to catch my performance. More important for Lacey, Mother was cutting her off from Levi. That might just be her breaking point.

Lacey had agreed not to push the issue of going out on a date with Levi until after Texapalooza. She did it for Levi, and she did it for me. Lacey kept her passion for cosmetology to herself probably because it was easier for her to slowly fail at singing than to let our mother down. Lacey, it seemed, gave up a lot of herself for other people. She had a problem saying no. However, at some point, yes becomes an impossible response. Lacey had finally hit that wall.

"Bible college!" She sat in front of her salon mirror without a lick of makeup on. "What am I going to major in? Snake handling?" She took a sucker out of a drawer. "I need a smoke."

"You don't need to smoke." I wanted to shake her. "You need to go tell Mother you're done singing, that you've thought for a long time about beauty school."

Lacey took a long pull at the sucker then popped it from her mouth with a smack. "You know she'll be up Saturday morning early. Both of us can't leave." Lacey's eyes reddened. She wanted to see Levi play and be there for me. Not going burned her up. "You can still ride with the guys, right?"

"Yes." I leaned against her dresser.

"Covering for you is the best I can do." Lacey growled, "Go for it, Paisley. Don't let those boys upstage you."

I picked up a fat blush brush and tapped the handle. "Are you going to the choir tryouts?"

"Hell, yeah." Lacey began twisting her hair into a bun. "And I'm going full-on Pentecostal—denim skirt, tennis shoes, and no makeup. Lacey Tillery in her best Bible-thumping camo."

"Lacey, Bible college really isn't that backward."

"I'm not dressing for the school. I'm dressing for Mother. She never once asked me if I wanted to go to sing in that choir. She just came home and told me what to do and where to do it. And she's going to pay dearly for messing up my plans."

"She'll never let you out of the house like that."

"Of course not. But by the time the fight is over, you'll be halfway to Austin. She won't even know you're gone."

29

SPIT-SHINED AND READY

Uncle L. V. pretended to rid *Miss Molly Moonlight* of any imperfections she might've picked up on her last air-show outing. He clutched a can of wax and dabbed at her aluminum sides with a cotton cloth. *Miss Molly* didn't have a blemish on her. L. V. just conjured up a reason to witness the Waylon Slider Band's final rehearsal before Texapalooza.

I put everything I had into the crash cymbal at the end of our set. That was the plan. We'd all end together on the high side: Waylon, Levi, and Cal bending the frets, Paradise with a wicked stretch of his accordion, me making the crash sing. We put everything we could rally, all we had on the top shelf. The high pitch rang throughout the hangar, all but lifting the roof off.

"Yeah, I like that." L. V. stopped his fake waxing. He'd listened to the whole set, start to finish. "Like the dark blues start and the bright end. You write all that, Waylon?"

"Me and Cal." Waylon ran his hand down the neck of his old Strat. "What about Paisley hand counting us in on the Latin drum?" He needed some outside assurance that opening with the *caja* would work.

"A bare hand on an animal-skin drum?" Uncle L. V. dropped the cotton cloth on the back of the chair and patted his chest twice. "That's native, son. It'll crawl up in you and hang on."

Paradise glanced at me with a half smile, but he kept his thoughts to himself. We all did. Even Levi had his game face on. For him taking the stage would be just like taking the pitcher's mound. And Cal. More so than anyone, Cal grasped the goal every time he grabbed his guitar. One and the same. The time for talking and analyzing and trying something new had passed. We'd planned the work, now we had to work the plan. We were ready. Waylon had us ready.

We watched Waylon cradle his Strat in the case as if he were laying a baby in a crib.

"Waylon"—L. V. picked up the waxing cloth and began folding it, edge to edge, until it was a small square—"your daddy showin' up?"

"Already there." Waylon closed the lid on the guitar and smoothed his hands across the top. "Been there all week with my uncle. Performing at different events. The producer, Lloyd Maines, has them in the studio playing on some artist's new record." Waylon flicked the handle on the case. "He can't afford not to show up when his name is on the band list."

My heart broke for Waylon. Split open. Even my mother had believed in Lacey despite her cratering at the rodeo. Mother blamed the bad performance on everything and everybody but Lacey. From what I'd seen at church, Waylon would never be good enough to get his father's approval. It was clear Waylon didn't think so either.

Levi and Cal were packed up and headed out. But Levi seemed to understand Waylon's circumstance better than anyone. "It's just you and the guitar, dude." Levi clinched his left hand into a fist as if it held a baseball. "Block out the crowd. Block out the pressure. Can't nobody do what you do, but you." Levi turned around on his way out the door. He made sure L. V. heard him. "I'll have the Tucker wine wagon gassed up, and I'll be down there by the bridge at five in the morning. We'll give you till five fifteen, Paisley." Levi waited to see if Uncle L. V. would object.

L. V. would let it go and he'd let me go. This was my deal and he wouldn't interfere. He and Waylon and Paradise stared at me.

"What?" I tried to play it off like showing up was nothing. "I'll be there. You just be on time."

"Lock her up, Paisley." Uncle L. V. grabbed his wax can. "I'm leaving for a bit."

Paradise slung his murse over his shoulder. "I'll see you tomorrow," he told me. "I need to catch your uncle. Talk him into loaning me a hat."

"Yeah, good luck with that." I chuckled at the idea that Paradise thought he could schmooze one of L. V.'s Colombian hats from his collection. I handed him my *caja*. "I can't hide this at home." The animal skin was warm from being played. I didn't want to let it go. "Make sure it makes the trip."

Paradise took the drum. I trusted him. Maybe even with my own heart.

Then I saw Waylon. Hands still spread on top of his guitar case. Head bowed. I think he was praying.

Everyone cleared out. Waylon and I were alone.

Waylon gathered his guitar and tucked his band notebook under his arm. He waited while I slid the hangar doors shut. One. Last. Time. I walked with him outside.

"Don't stand me up, Paisley." He laid the guitar in the backseat of his car. "You lead us off. You set the pace. We're all screwed without you."

I knew that was hard for Waylon to admit. "No worries." I was more confident in my ability to get there than I was in his ability to perform. "Nothing can keep me from Austin."

The cool winds of March and April had died down. The early May evening was as still as dawn. The only movement was a buzzard circling high over the rolling pasture and a jarring racket from the front side of the hangar.

Tires sailing over gravel.

Skidding to a stop.

A familiar door squawking open and slamming shut.

The *click-shh-click-shh* of stilettos tottering across the gravel toward us.

Waylon gripped his steering wheel to pull himself into his old Camaro, oblivious to the sound of someone arriving.

"Don't," I said. Grabbed his arm.

The thought of Mother finding the drums, figuring out about the band iced me in the moment. She'd never approve. She'd blame the drums for any ill she could think of and forbid me to play. I could not lose the drums. I couldn't.

In a split second, I made a choice. The only thing I knew would keep her from nosing around, finding the drums. Keep her from any hint of my going to Texapalooza.

As Mother rounded the corner of the hangar, I seized Waylon's head in my hands. "Kiss me, Waylon."

30

GIMME THREE STEPS

On a scale of one to ten, the kiss was a two. Too sudden. Too hard. Waylon stayed so tense all the time that his naturally thin lips cracked from dryness. It was like rubbing my lips across the scales of a fish. When I turned him loose, Waylon kept his mouth pinched tight and his nose turned up as if he'd gotten a whiff of a skunk. A sentiment I shared.

But the kiss worked.

Mother shrieked like a swamp witch, *"EeeeeEEEEEEEEEE!"*

From the corner of my eye, I saw her: hands to her face, pink satin blouse shimmering in the sun, capri jeans squeezing her in like a sausage casing, pink platform stilettos.

I straightened Waylon's skull cap. In the fury of the moment, my grip on his head had pulled the cap nearly over his eyes. "Go." I shoved him inside his old Camaro. He caught a glimpse of my mother and fumbled for his keys. "Drive off now."

Waylon cranked his car and charged into the pasture. Away from the drive between the house and the hangar. Away from my mother. His tires laid the tall grass flat, cutting a trail through the pasture.

I steadied my resolve for whatever drama she'd rain down on me. I could take it. She'd be swinging at a ghost. I'd be on my way to Austin. But when I turned to face my mother, she was gone. Disappeared.

I ran around the hangar in time to see Mother's Suburban hightail it across the pasture. Making a beeline for the fence. Hammer down. She was cutting Waylon off before he could leave the farm.

The ground under my feet shook and so did I. She was going after him. I never planned on that.

As Waylon raced for the gate, Mother shot like a dart in front of him. The broad side of the Suburban a bull's-eye for the Camaro.

I ran hard down the gravel drive toward them. "STOP! STOP IT!"

In a sharp instant, the Camaro's engine whined down, the pipes backfired and popped, and Waylon cut the wheel, angling the car within a whisker of clipping the Suburban's front bumper. When he got in front of her, Waylon took off again. Pouring on the gas. Shredding the clover in the pasture. His wide back wheels firing red buds and dirt clods onto the Suburban—*thwonk-thwonk-thwonk-thwonk*—pummeling the hood. Waylon circled trying to lose her.

Mother chased him. Rode his bumper around and around and around, nose to tail, until finally Waylon drifted onto the driveway, catching traction on the gravel. The Camaro's engine roared as he sped across the cattle drive and skidded onto the blacktop county road. He smoked the tires and laid a line of rubber twenty yards long.

Mother's Suburban rattled toward the gate. The taillights flickered as she bounced across the cattle guard. She paused at the road. I could see her watching Waylon disappear over the rolling hills. The hum of his car engine fading like the end of a song. Mother turned the Suburban toward home.

In the cloud of engine smoke and burning smell of rubber, I stared at the mess in Uncle L. V.'s pasture. A mess I created. I stood there on the gravel measuring every deep rut and smashed clover bud. Mother and Waylon could've both been hurt. Badly. And L. V.'s neat farm was carved up in doughnut circles. He'd make me replant that field and nurse it until every single blade of grass grew back.

Dad's words about getting in a bad situation and not staying there and wallowing in it hit home. Things were more complicated than I ever imagined they could become. Still, all I needed was one more day. Less than twenty-four hours. Just one more day.

I wanted to talk to Paradise, but I knew what he'd say too. "Wide-open. You gotta live wide-open."

I rode the four-wheeler home through the thicket to face whatever I had coming. I'd cover up what I had to. Wide-open would have to wait.

31

A SLICE OF TRUTH

With all the steadiness and precision of a diamond cutter, Mother laid the sharp sawing blades of her electric knife right where the bread crust meets the soft white center. She severed it. Tossing the crust to the side.

Lacey must've been working on her Pentecostal outfit because her hair was formed into a tidy, virginal bun, and she'd zipped herself into a long denim skirt that nearly covered her ankles. She'd run into the kitchen in a hurry. Except for her hot pink bra, Lacey was topless and almost breathless.

"I told her she was nuts, but Mother swears she saw you making out with Waylon Slider."

I rolled my eyes. Reached down to pull off my boots. Mother was going to draw that one kiss into an entire relationship; I counted on it. The less I acted like I cared, the sooner I might be able to put it behind me. Regardless, I could deal with whatever punishment she'd lay down when I got back from Austin.

"It was one kiss." I tugged a boot off. "And she tried to kill him."

Mother stacked another tower of pimento cheese sandwiches.

Hit the power button on the knife. The shrill whine filled the kitchen. "I'm not done with that boy either." She drove the knife into the bread, cutting away the crusts. "I'm sure he thinks he can strum some on his guitar and girls will just start flinging their panties at him. Not my girls. No way."

I almost laughed. If I was sure of anything, it was that thought never occurred to Waylon, and I was no panty flinger.

Mother stopped carving. She rested the knife and pressed both hands palms down on the table. She closed her eyes. "Paisley, I'm only going to ask you this one time. Did you sin with him?"

"I don't even know how to answer that." I tugged off my other boot and sat both by the door. They'd be ready when I headed out in the morning.

"Don't smart off to me, Paisley." Mother placed her perfectly carved finger sandwiches on a platter. "I know you've run off some-where with him at least once. I went by L. V.'s. You weren't there. What were you doing that you had to run off somewhere to do it?"

"So instead of asking where I was the day you moved my drumsticks"—I wanted her to know that I knew she'd been there. She wasn't spotless—"you thought you'd just catch me. You got what you were looking for."

Lacey picked up one of the sandwiches.

Mother turned on her. "Don't you act like you're innocent either. I saw your car up there earlier in the week."

Lacey's mouth fell open. "Paisley, did you steal my car to go see Waylon Slider?" She bit the little sandwich in half. Lacey obviously saw no need in both of us taking the heat.

So I shouldered that lie too. "This has nothing to do with Lacey."

Mother's voice went high and nasally. "I don't know what I'm going to do with you, Paisley." She arranged the white bread sandwiches along with pumpernickel finger sandwiches so that they looked like a platter full of piano keys. "Sneaking around. Lying. With that gosh-awful Waylon Slider." Mother officially teared up. "Why can't you girls be interested in some nice boys like"—she sniffled as she stacked—"those boys whose daddy owns the Ford dealership in Big Wells?"

Lacey nearly choked on that suggestion. She coughed and coughed until she could pour a glass of water. All Mother knew about those boys was that they had money and community clout. In her mind, those two characteristics trumped farm boys any day of the week.

Mother patted her eyes with a corner of her apron. "I want people looking up to you girls. Not down."

"Not that it matters, but it was one kiss." I opened up. "I'm not interested in another one. But Waylon and I are friends. He's not going anywhere."

"Well, neither are you." Mother powered up the electric knife again and went hard after another stack of sandwiches. "My prayer has been that you'd find your passion, find something you loved to do and could work at in school. Something that would get you out of Prosper County." She slapped pimento cheese spread onto a slice of bread. "That's my dumb luck for praying for you to find your passion."

Lacey cut her eyes at me. Without their usual embellishments of caked-on color, Lacey's eyes looked as hollow as I felt.

RURAL AND RESTLESS

From the bridge that crosses Cypress Creek, you can
watch the water run.
> That old creek lays low, runs deep
> But it can flow beyond its banks.
> It may be quiet now, but not for long. It's rural
> and restless.

The old courthouse darkens the Big Wells square, still
I take my board to town.
> Airwalk down the steps, nose grind on
> the handrails
> Until the cops bust the ride
> Outsiders killing small-town time. We're all rural
> and restless.

I've known for a while this county can't hold me, like it
can't hold Cypress Creek.
> One day I'll pack my songs, my guitar.
> Consider myself blessed.
> I know where I'm from, taking that with me.
> I'm rural and restless.

32

WIDE-OPEN

Darkness is its own kind of illuminator. Shades of gray, black, midnight blue stirred ghost-like in my room. I slipped into my favorite cutoffs, a tank, a hoodie. The moon, sneaking between the curtains, cast a haunting silver light on my dresser, my drumsticks, the ring my parents gave me. Mother actually thought I'd have sex with Waylon. That's what she thought of me. She didn't know me at all. I suppose I didn't give her much to work with.

I opened my bedroom door, stopping just before the hinge squeaked. The hall, lined with pageant pictures and pretty little-girl portraits of me and Lacey, even some of Dad in his baseball glory days, was as inviting as a cold black funeral car. And then there were the pictures of Mother: a twirler in a blue sequined leotard and white patent-leather go-go boots, the baseball star's girl in a princess-cut prom dress that hid her waist. A few steps in, I stopped by Lacey's room—her door ajar. My sister was curled into a ball somewhere under the mound of bedcovers. She'd draped her Pentecostal costume over a chair. The salon mirror reflected nothing but the opaque early morning and her hidden dream.

My boots sat by the kitchen door. Right where I left them. I picked them up and turned around one last time. Tray after tray of music-note cookies covered the kitchen table. The piano-key finger sandwiches were somewhere in the fridge. Mother was ready to go. Ready to take Lacey to perform a lie. Believing one hundred percent in absolutely nothing.

I turned the knob, almost waiting for someone to stop me. Dad would step out any minute. Or Mother.

No one came.

The path was wide-open.

Leaving was easy.

I opened the door. The chilly morning air sent goose bumps crawling up my legs. I waited, thinking that was it. They probably heard me.

No one came.

Dad's baseball cap hung from a cabinet knob. He'd be up for coffee before long. I'd be gone.

I shut the door behind me, stepped into my boots in the garage.

The moonlight, although scarce and tucked behind the clouds, shed enough light for me to find my way across the pasture. I hiked through the almost-knee-high grass and over the groundsel-covered rolling hills. The darkness camouflaged the bright gold flower clusters and passed them off as dull yellow weeds. A ghostly mist floated in the distance, hovering over the creek and Moon Lake. The night sky seemed to stretch on forever and so did Prosper County. The hills swelled and plunged as far as I could see. Where one grove of bushy trees stopped, another started. When Mother went off about Prosper County, she talked like it had walls. This morning Prosper County had no boundaries. No end to the countryside in sight.

Coming up on the deer run leading into the thicket between our place and Uncle L. V.'s, I missed the four-wheeler. The black trail snaked through the thicket, and I thought about running it. It's easier to be fearless getting through the woods on a four-wheeler. On the other side, where the thicket opens to the pasture, L. V.'s hangar waited as did the boys, the band on the bridge.

God turned up the morning volume. The sun was still below the horizon, but the dark morning had brightened to the color of new denim. The whistling of spring birds livened up the pasture. I could see our yellow house behind me. Still. Quiet. Not a light on.

For what seemed like forever, I'd chased my dream to drum, to leave Prosper County, over the trail to the hangar, and now Austin and Texapalooza waited for me just on the other side. All I had to do was hit that trail one last time. One foot in front of the other. Everything had worked out just like I planned. Except for the nagging, creeping feeling that I was leaving something behind. I checked my back pocket. My drumsticks were there. What I left wasn't something I could carry. It was the thing that carried me.

I stopped.

Pushing forward would've been easier.

I took a few steps backward, away from the trail, through the high grass. The blades tickled my calves and the thicket shrank as I pulled back. I knew Paradise would understand. Levi too. Waylon and Cal maybe not.

I turned for home. Wide-open was the only way to live.

33

TRUTH HURTS

Mother stood motionless for a minute before the sack she was clutching fell from her arms. Lemons bounced and scattered across the kitchen floor. Mother grabbed her stomach. "My God, Paisley." She closed her eyes, dropped her head, and muttered, "You've been out all night."

I wasn't sure if she meant that as a question or an observation. She might've even meant it as a prayer.

"It's not what you think," I said.

"Then what is it?" Dad weaved his belt through the loops of his jeans. "Your boots are wet."

"The dew in the pasture." I felt a fear welling with every boiling drag of the coffeemaker.

Mother shrieked, "He just dumped you out in the pasture?"

"No. No one dumped me anywhere." My throat tightened. This was going all wrong. "I came back to tell you." I looked at my dad, the scar on his left shoulder. He'd chased his dream wide-open with a stadium full of family and friends. They were there when he started and there when it ended. I was tired of going it alone.

"I came back so you could take me to Austin." I knew when I said that, it was a game changer. I didn't know what would happen, but it couldn't be worse than keeping everything in. I was letting it go and letting it out. Finally free. Like spinning in a circle on the pier at Moon Lake with Paradise.

"Austin?" Mother sank onto a chair.

Dad stood behind her with his hands on her shoulders.

"There's nothing between me and Waylon." I took a deep breath. "Except his band."

Mother's eyes hardened. She reached for Dad's hand on her shoulder.

No point in holding back. The sun was coming up, and we had a six-hour drive ahead of us.

"I'm the drummer for the Waylon Slider Band. We play"—I swallowed hard—"we play Texapalooza tonight in Austin. I was headed across the pasture to meet up with the band."

Mother glanced at the trays of music-note cookies, at the kitchen window, at the sink. She squeezed Dad's hand. I think she'd convinced herself that she was deep in sleep and trying to climb out of a bad dream.

I carried on with what I'd been thinking for weeks. "I don't want to run away to get there. I want someone in this family to take me."

Dad grabbed a cup and waited as the coffeepot gurgled and spit. "For a drummer, Paisley," he said, "you've got some off timing."

"A drummer?" Mother slapped both hands on the table, stood up. She was good and awake. "Drums! What do you know about drumming? A snare in the school band doesn't count. Kitchen pans and wooden spoons don't either. You've never had a professional lesson.

If Waylon Slider told you how good you were at drums and how you could be in his band, he was buttering you up because he wanted something." Mother bent down and snatched up the lemons. "From what I saw outside L. V.'s hangar, it looks like Waylon is well on his way to getting it."

Dad drank his coffee. He'd blow a cooling breath across the top then take a sip. Blow and sip. Blow and sip. One. Two. Three. Four. Just like I'd count the band in on my *caja*. If we could get there on time.

"The only thing Waylon wants from me is to play the drums. We've been practicing in Uncle L. V.'s hangar. I use that old drum kit."

Mother palmed a lemon. I think she wanted to throw it at me. "I kissed Waylon so you'd not ask me why I was there."

Mother slammed the lemon down, jerked a cutting board and carving knife from a drawer. "Oh, what a tangled web you weave." She slit the lemon in half, then cut it with lightning speed into perfect wedges, gritting her teeth. "When once you practice to deceive."

Through the kitchen window, I saw the pasture with its wildflower-covered hills come to light in the morning sun. If I was going to make Austin, we needed to hit the road.

"Mother, I didn't run off this morning when I could have. I may have made some mistakes, but I'm owning up to them. And I've got to get to Austin." I looked down at my boots, the dark stained edges from the wet grass. I had to trust that turning around and coming home could not have been a mistake. Goodwill had to be on my side. "The band is counting on me."

"Hah." Mother shook her head and carved her lemons. "I can't believe we've raised you to be so gullible. Waylon Slider is going to get his little hick hiney handed to him on a really big stage." Mother loaded handfuls of lemon wedges into a plastic bag. "And I'm going to protect you from that humiliation."

Dad folded his arms at his waist. I'd seen him do that in baseball games when the pitcher was losing a batter and throwing junk balls instead of strikes. Settle down. Focus.

"You let people look down on you. I don't care. I'm not ashamed of where I'm from or what I do and neither is Waylon. We're playing our style of music, and folks can take it or leave it. It's an under-eighteen competition. We're actually better than you think." My voice cracked from the fear that I was about to be stuck at home during Texapalooza, but I forced myself to stay the course. "I can explain everything to you on the way to Austin. I just really need for you, for somebody, to take me."

Mother began placing the bags of sliced lemons and trays of cookies into a large plastic box labeled THE KITCHEN GODDESS. "Paisley Tillery." She used both names—not a good sign. "I can't even process all that you've snuck around behind my back and done. I don't want to even think about it. And I am certainly not of a mind to take you to the end of the driveway much less a six-hour drive to Austin or anywhere else. And even if I was, which let me make clear I am *not*, I have a catering job today. And your sister has tryouts for a choir today. Have you even stopped to think what that means to her?" Mother's voice grew louder and louder. "And you want us to throw away Lacey's future—her college plans—so that you can go bang on a drum and help Waylon Slider make a fool of himself and you too?"

Dad stayed silent and kept his arms at his waist. But I had stayed calm as long as I could. My dream, my commitment to the band, everything was rolling away from me—faster and faster downhill. I had to catch it.

I pulled my sticks from my back pocket. Laid them on the table in front of her, in the big middle of all her handy catering work done for a dream Lacey didn't even have. "My dream is important too." I kept my hand on the sticks. "I have to get to Austin."

Mother iced the plan. "The only thing you have to get is a grip on reality."

I grabbed my sticks. "NO!" I looked at Dad. "Someone has to take me."

"It isn't about the ride, Paisley," he said. "It's about the blessing."

He was right. I had wanted Mother's blessing, her presence. I had a crazy notion that playing in a band was a stupid thing to hide, and everyone else's family could be on board so why not mine. But not anymore. Now I just wanted, needed, to get to Austin. "I trusted that if I turned around and did the right thing, came back, you'd under-stand. Y'all have always said you'd support us. I'm telling you drum-ming in this contest is my dream. I've worked my butt off for it. Give me a break. Give me the same effort you give Lacey."

Mother closed her eyes and shook her head as if I was the one being difficult. "Stop with the selfishness," she said. "We'll talk about this later. Right now we've got to focus on Lacey and the tryouts."

I thought I'd scream. Until I heard Lacey's voice behind me. "I'm not going to those tryouts."

I spun around.

Lacey stepped into the kitchen in her pink pajamas, her hair pushed back in a headband. She held an envelope out to Mother. The GLAMOUR BEAUTY COLLEGE logo in the top left corner.

"Lacey, no." I tried to stop her. Good intentions seemed to be punished in this house. I didn't want Lacey to screw up her chances.

Mother opened the envelope. Dad moved behind her, read over her shoulder. "Beauty school?"

"Yep." Lacey yawned. "I'm doin' hair and makeup. I'm done with singing." She took a Diet Coke from the fridge and popped the top. As if it were any other typical morning.

Mother handed the letter to Dad. She spoke carefully to Lacey. "You're giving up too easily and settling for so much less than what you deserve."

Dad pointed at the letter. "It says here you've been approved for financial aid." He seemed to take that part personally. "Since when do you need financial aid?"

Lacey took a swig of her soda. She fished underneath the plastic wrap and pulled out a quarter-note cookie. "I wasn't taking any chances."

"Chances!" Mother took off her kitchen goddess apron, crumpled it into a wad, and threw it on a chair. "This is your future. You have no idea the chance you're taking. Your dad and I have scrimped and saved so you girls could get an education and make a better life for yourselves. And your bright idea is to make a career standing on your feet twelve hours a day, listening to customers complain because their haircut doesn't match the magazine picture, and nursing your hands dry and beet red from soap and water and chemicals?"

Lacey smiled. "That is so my bright idea."

Mother stared at Lacey, then she looked me over from my drumsticks to my boots. "God help us all."

Sunlight filled the kitchen. If I didn't find a way to get to Austin soon, we'd be running into traffic and risk missing the show.

"Let me get this straight." Dad still held on to the beauty college letter. "You took it upon yourself to apply for financial aid before asking me about that?"

As usual, the conversation centered on what Lacey was or was not going to do while the clock ticked away on my performance.

"I'll still need help paying for school." Lacey offered that as if it would make him feel better. "I want a degree in business too. So I can have my own salon one day."

Mother pulled the platters of finger sandwiches from the refrigerator. In the morning sunlight, the purple discs under each of her eyes made her look like she'd been punched. "I've done all this." Her eyes reddened. "And you knew the whole time you weren't singing."

Lacey had Dad's coolness. She could sit a batter down. "I told you after the rodeo I was done singing." Lacey snapped a cookie in half and popped a piece in her mouth. "You just hear what you want to hear."

I rolled a drumstick through my fingers, end over end and back again. I stood it as long as I could. "I'm running out of time. If no one is taking me, can I please have the keys to drive myself?"

Mother took a deep breath and looked at Dad. "The only person going anywhere is me. I still have catering to deliver." She snatched up one of the boxes. "You two can stay home and make up grand schemes to carry out behind our backs."

Lacey tried to help me. "You can be mad at me, but Paisley deserves to get to play in Austin. If I was her, I'd be two hours down the road by now."

"The only thing you two deserve is each other." Mother threw open the kitchen door and headed for the Suburban.

I pleaded with Dad. "You know I've worked for this. I came back. I told the truth."

"Sometimes you can be too late with the truth."

"You could take me." My heart swelled with every beat. My chest heaved. *"Please."*

"Don't ask me to go against your momma. I've loved her since she was your age. You two act like you're the only ones who ever wanted anything out of life. She sacrificed her wants so that the rest of us could go after ours, and she did it while bearing the weight of her own friends and family treating her like trash, excluding her. And now you're going to fault her for wanting better for you than what she had. For wanting people to respect you. Let me tell you two something. She never gave up and walked away from me when things got rough. I ain't turnin' my back on her now." He picked up a box and opened the door. "You shouldn't give up on her either. There'll be other band shows."

The door closed behind him.

I stood perfectly still. The water faucet over the sink dripped. *Plink. Plink. Plink.* "I shouldn't have come back." I said it to myself but Lacey was listening.

"Dumb ass." Lacey broke another cookie. "But I texted Levi when I heard y'all in here talking. He said Waylon had a backup plan. His uncle will fill in for you."

That burned like a hornet sting. I wasn't surprised. I suppose I was relieved. But I was the drummer for the Waylon Slider Band. It was *my* job. And Waylon's uncle was too old. The band would get to play, but they'd probably get disqualified.

I looked through the small window in the kitchen door. Mother and Dad were sitting on the bumper of the Suburban. She leaned against his arm and clutched his hand between her knees. I watched her wipe away tears with the back of her hand. The tears were probably for Lacey.

"I'm not going to Austin."

It sounded so unreal. Even if Dad was talking to her and somehow Mother changed her mind, too much time had gone by. We'd never make it. "I'm, I'm not going to Austin," I repeated.

I glanced through the little window in the kitchen door one last time. Dad had her wrapped in his arms. She might come around, but it was too late for me.

I'd been on my bed for over an hour, staring at the wall, playing Texapalooza over and over in my head for what seemed forever. Waylon's uncle wouldn't attempt the *caja*. They'd go for the sure thing and open with a straight snare count. He'd set the pace, probably even throughout the whole set. Could be a yawner, but Paradise on his accordion would add some interest. They'd skip the drum solo, my solo.

The door to my room opened. I didn't roll over. I didn't care who it was. Lacey knew better than to bother me. But from the heavy scent of sweet perfume, I knew it was Mother.

"Paisley, I'm going to deliver the catering. When I get back, we can talk about this thing, this whatever you have for playing the drums."

She waited.

I kept my thoughts to myself.

"Don't think I don't care about your dreams," she said. "If I could change things for you, I would. I'm not saying I'd approve. I'll never allow you to hang out with a bunch of . . . I'm just saying I'll dig down deep. We'll find a way to support you and the dreams that you have." She sounded like she was simply repeating the words Dad would've told her.

I pulled a pillow into my chest. The heels of my boots clicked together. I'd forgotten I even had them on. When the anger eased, I simply went cold.

"I know that playing on that stage was a really big deal to you." Mother tapped the toe of her high heel. "Even though I don't think you and that Slider boy have a clue that there is a process. You have to work up to doing something like playing in Austin."

I hugged the pillow. "That's the problem. You think there's some hierarchy because of how folks around here treated you. And you think because we're rural we're somehow automatically at the bottom of the ladder. That's not how I see the world. I'm not looking up or looking down. I'm looking forward."

"If I'd known about this band showcase sooner, if you'd given me a chance, I would've given you a chance. But I can't sprout wings and take you there."

I sat straight up. She might not have wings, but we could still get to Austin. Mother's heels clicked down the hallway. *CLICK. Click. click.*

I ran after her. "Do you mean that? If you had a chance you'd take me?"

Her eyes were swollen from all that Lacey and I had done. "I'd make sure you got to live your dream."

34

A DREAM TAKES FLIGHT

Uncle L. V. backed his tractor up to the hangar. Dad hooked a bar behind *Miss Molly Moonlight*'s nosewheel. When L. V. slowly tugged her out, *Miss Molly* rolled into the sunlight with a promising smile. Guaranteed to please. The Prosper County countryside shined on her aluminum sides. L. V. parked her at one end of the grass runway.

He climbed down from the tractor. His shirt was missing its sleeves, and he had a do-rag and sunglasses on. He stared up at the sun. "We better set out for Austin," he said. "She ain't the Concorde."

Mother, in her stilettos, carefully stepped through the grass. Her purse, which was the size of a large shopping bag, threw her balance off and she teetered. "Gosh, L. V. As much as you fly, you'd think you'd concrete a runway."

"If you don't hush, I'm going to put you in the gun turret." He pointed at the clear globe on *Miss Molly*'s roof. "After what you did to my pasture, I'm a hair away from dropping both you and Paisley over Jessup County anyway."

Dad smiled. He and Lacey stood by the runway as Mother, L. V., and I got ready to leave.

I hugged Dad. "I wish you could come."

"Someone's got to be the kitchen goddess and deliver that catering." He grabbed Lacey and cuddled us both in a bear hug. "And Lacey is going to help me figure out what I need to do to get her school paid for."

I stepped toward the plane.

Lacey reached up and tidied my hair. "Put on some lip gloss before you go on," she said. "Mother's got a purse full of product. If you get a chance, put some gel in Levi's hair. Just a dab. He doesn't like it goopy."

"I will."

"And give him a good-luck kiss, but tell him it's from me."

"OK, I will," I said. Mother was going to love that.

"And Paisley"—Lacey grabbed both my hands—"don't you let those boys outshine you." She squeezed so hard my fingers throbbed. "You own that stage."

I climbed into the plane and sat in the copilot seat next to L. V. I hadn't ridden with him in a long time, but I put on the headphones and belted in as if I'd done it yesterday. It was time to fly.

Dad helped boost Mother in, and she landed on the hull where in wartime the bombs were loaded and dropped.

Uncle L. V.'s voice came through headphones. "The drop bay works, Diane."

He flipped the master switch and the panel in front of him lit up.

The green runway stretched before us. It always seemed longer from inside the plane.

With the tip of his finger, Uncle L. V. flicked switches. When he pressed *Miss Molly*'s starter buttons, the propellers spun and the engines fired up. A loud BOOM and a puff of black smoke, and *Miss Molly* turned on with the deep, rumbling growl of a pack of Harleys.

I turned around to make sure Mother was still with us. She was buckled in and praying.

We bumped and rolled down the runway. Faster and faster. The trees in the thicket turned into one gray blur. Then I felt it. The lift. *Miss Molly* with the rush of wind under her belly defying gravity and soaring higher and higher.

Uncle L. V. tilted her wings and circled Dripping Springs—our little rural patch of Prosper County. Up this high and in the distance, I could see the Tucker Barn with its Texas flag roof. L. V. dipped *Miss Molly* low toward his pasture. The rings of tire tracks from Mother's and Waylon's chase scarred L. V.'s otherwise perfectly groomed clover patch. He rounded the pasture again.

"I'll get right on that when we get back." I watched him out of the corner of my eye. He nodded and leaned into the throttle, pushing *Miss Molly* to the southwest toward Austin.

Mother sat on the bomb hatch and sipped on a Diet Sprite when L. V. wasn't looking. Flying to Austin so that I could play Texapalooza wasn't easy on her. But she was hanging in like a champ, just like Dad said she would.

Below us, yellow patches of wildflowers cut between lush green groves and pools of water. From this high, Moon Lake curved in a perfect crescent. The day was full and bright—the perfect setting to live out a dream. *Miss Molly*'s engines hummed and puttered. She had her own voice. I took it all in, wanting to remember every single sound, every single vibration as we cruised in the blue sky.

I watched the landscape change through the side window and

the windshield until a couple hours passed and the dome on the Texas state capitol rose out of the hill country. When we flew around the outskirts of downtown Austin, I took in the crowds of folks gathered around the convention center.

Uncle L. V.'s voice cracked in the headphones. "Stubb's Bar-B-Que." He pointed to a row of old brick buildings. Everybody from Willie Nelson to George Clinton played that joint.

"No bar playing." Mother's voice came through loud and clear.

I'd probably wait for another day to go wide-open with her about our gig at Don Caliente's Taco Bar and Cantina.

The Texapalooza outdoor stages, three, maybe four, where the bands played—where I'd play—dotted downtown.

Uncle L. V. radioed the airport tower. "November One-Nine-Four-One Prosper County Home requesting to land."

I played out a slap stroke on the tops of my thighs. Making sure I could still do it. I mean, I knew how to do it. I knew that. I just needed to remind myself, feel the rub and stroke. *Miss Molly* settled on the runway, and it was my time to take off and soar.

35

GRAVITY

The shuttle let us out next to a mime—some dude and his stringless guitar both painted chalk white. My Texapalooza welcome was a clown. A fake guitar-playing, weirdo mime. A pretender. Maybe that's why I hated clowns. They were just madeup people trying to be something they're not and putting on a show.

Standing on the downtown curb by the park, the hum of the festival crowd and the smell of grilled onions from a hot dog stand overloaded my senses.

For May, the air turned thick with humidity. I took off my hoodie and tied it around my waist. I cupped my hands over my mouth. *Huff. Huff. Huff.* Deep breaths. But the mime and the onions and my nerves knotted in my gut. What if we were all just a bunch of clowns? Including Paradise and his squeezebox.

"That tank top cannot be your performance outfit." Mother seemed oblivious to the fact that I was close to passing out.

No way could I hold a costume conversation with her.

Mother reached in her purse and pulled out her bottle of Diet Sprite. "Drink this." She had her black, bug-eyed sunglasses on. I was so dizzy I thought I saw two of her. Like giant bouffant-haired horseflies buzzing around me and the mime.

"We didn't come all this way for you to be too puny to play," she said.

I took a small sip. This day had been like trying to get a drink of water from a fire hydrant.

"Paisley." Uncle L. V. pulled my drumsticks from my back pocket. "Hold on to these."

The sun had warmed the wood. The sticks stuck to my sweaty hand. I dried them on my cutoffs and turned my back on the mime. When those sticks hit my palm, I remembered all I could do. All I was in Austin to do. And the boys' guitars had real strings. And nothing about Paradise was fake. We were the real deal.

I pulled myself together. "This way."

Uncle L. V. and Mother followed me to a roped-off area behind an outdoor stage. I knew it had to be the one. KICK FM radio sponsored the Texapalooza youth showcase. Their signs were plastered all around. The morning personalities and band showcase judges—Colt Collins and his sidekick, Jaybird—were broadcasting live.

A young guy in a neon yellow vest that read STAFF guarded the backstage. He had earphones in and was playing air guitar.

"I'm with one of the bands." I pointed at Mother and L. V. I spoke loud and slow as if that would help him hear me. "They're. With. Me."

"You. Don't. Have. A. Wristband." He mimicked me, never missed a chord in his air solo.

"I'm late." I shuddered. He might not let us through. "C'mon."

"No can do, babe."

Mother bumped him with her big purse. "Listen here, Junior." She motioned for me to duck under the rope. "She's the drummer for the band, the Waylon Slider Band." Mother waved her arms. The jingle-clinking of her bracelets distracted the guard long enough that I ducked under the rope and headed for the stage. Afraid to look back, I could hear Mother carrying on. "Slider? Doesn't that name ring a bell with you, Mr. Guitar Player?"

She'd weasel her way in. I was sure of it. If not, Uncle L. V. would flex some muscle.

I worked my way through the bands behind the stage. The *twang* and *plunk* of guitars tuning. A fiddle, maybe two, dancing in the thick air. A splitting screech from an electric guitar. Cymbals crash-ing. The cacophony of sounds bounced around me until my heart settled on one sizzling whine—drawn-out lonesome and hanging high pitch above the rest.

My heart leapt three steps ahead of my feet.

Paradise and his smokin' squeezebox.

I searched the crowd of kids—some dressed up like Sunday church, some wearing Spandex pop-tart outfits. A tall girl in plat-form pumps and a shiny dress lost her balance and fell into me.

I took a few steps sideways. Tried to look around her. As if lifted by the wind, my feet left the ground. But I knew the strength in the arms that wrapped around me, and I lost myself to the moment—the damp curls of his hair, the salty taste of sweat glistening on his neck, the sandpaper scruffiness of a shadow beard, and a kiss as sweet and suc-culent as a summer peach.

Paradise.

"You're late." He clutched me to him as if putting me down meant letting me go.

"I took a detour when I went wide-open," I said.

"Paisley!" Mother had her sunglasses off. She'd made it through security. "I suppose you're going to tell me this is not what I think it is?"

Paradise loosened his hold.

"No." I slid to the ground. No point in hiding the obvious truth. "This is what you think."

"I'm Gabe." He stuck his hand out.

Mother stared at Paradise. She had it in her to slap him if the notion struck her. But she checked her temper. Mother reached to shake his hand with a polite and icy smile. She inventoried the Colombian cowboy hat with the black-and-white rings. "L. V., is that your hat?"

Uncle L. V. slapped Paradise on the back. "Not anymore."

The late afternoon grew warm and muggy as a ceiling of clouds began to block the sun. Waylon and Cal marched toward us. Cal's long blond hair blew away from his face the faster he walked, and he had a blue bandana tied around his forehead.

Mother squinched her eyes at Cal, then whispered to me, "Tell me that boy is not wearing guyliner."

Waylon stopped way short of arm's length from my mother. "I need you, us, all by the stage." Waylon glanced at the stage. Colt Collins and Jaybird were standing on it doing an interview. An interview with Waylon's father. "As soon as they finish, the competition starts. We've got to be ready to go on quickly."

"Sorry I'm late," I told him.

Waylon dripped with sweat. "I really want to open with that *caja*." That was his way of saying he was glad I made it.

One of Waylon's uncles, the drummer, chimed in with his years of experience. "She hasn't been here to rehearse. It's better to get disqualified because of the drummer's age than risk a reputation with a sloppy timekeeper."

I could've nailed him in the crotch with the toe of my boot. That Slider bunch worried too much about protecting their precious family reputation. I felt Paradise slip a finger in a belt loop. But nothing held my mother back.

"A sloppy timekeeper? Pa-lease!" Mother held her purse by the handles as if she might wind up and fling it. "Don't you have a church band to go drum in?"

Uncle L. V. motioned for us all to head toward the stage. Mother followed behind us repeating, "Sloppy timekeeper, my backside," with every stomp of her stilettos.

Levi waited up ahead. Lacey must've warned him. He was staying as far from my mother as he could. The five of us—Waylon, Levi, Cal, Paradise, and me—drifted away from the family, away from the other bands, and huddled by the stage.

Colt Collins's voice rang out across the park. Whoops and clapping erupted as they announced the rules and the showcase kickoff.

"We play like we practice." Waylon kept us together, had us focused. The humidity turned downtown Austin into a sauna. "You're taking the stage first, Paisley. Count us in. Just like the hangar practice."

I could tell he needed assurance, and I needed to say it. "I've got it. No worries." A trickle of cool sweat slipped down my cleavage.

The first band hit the stage. The applause from the audience was lukewarm at best. Maybe it was the heat, but the band started slow and never got off the ground.

"Well, folks"—Levi turned his baseball cap backward—"wake me when they're done."

We all chuckled. Nervous laughter. I stood on my tiptoes and kissed his cheek. "That's from Lacey."

He looked over his shoulder for my mother. She and L. V. were making their way toward the audience from backstage, but she kept watch.

The first band finished and the second took the stage. All girls. Dressed to the hilt. And they rocked it out. Cal clapped and threw up a fist pump.

"Their guitars are on." Waylon watched the girls like a hawk. "But the vocals are screamy and the drummer's nothing special."

Paradise winked at me.

I'd always believed we had a shot to win, more than a good shot. Then Waylon's dad came over and pulled Waylon to the side. Held up his hand with his fingers stretched open. He tapped each finger as if he were counting reasons why Waylon would fail. By the time he got to his thumb, Waylon cut him off, "It's my name too."

Waylon walked away, back to us.

He picked up his '61 Strat, slipped it over his shoulder, tightened the leather strap. SLIDER.

"We're one band away from rockin' the hell out of this town." He gritted his teeth, and as burning hot as it was, Waylon slipped a skull cap on his head anyway. "Get ready."

My sticks were in my back pocket. Paradise handed me the *caja*. I brushed my hand across the skin. My toes curled in my boots.

Waylon called out, "Lead the way, Paisley."

I made my way to the steps to the stage. Paradise's family, Levi's older brothers, my mother, and L. V. stood side by side with the Sliders. That probably hadn't occurred since their high school years.

Mother fanned herself with a flyer. One arm of my hoodie hung out of her purse. I've never wanted to drum so badly in my life. The band before us cleared off and I took the stage. I raised the throne and moved the hi-hats closer to me. I threw a silent straight arm, just to make sure I had the reach. I held the *caja* between my legs and took a deep breath, as Colt Collins announced, "The Waylon Slider Band."

36

LIVIN' A DREAM

Under the heat from the stage lights and the sweltering humidity, I dripped from sweat. My bangs stuck to my forehead. The crowd, shoulders bumping shoulders, loomed in front of me. With the little drum between my legs, I drew a beat out of the *caja*. A rub. A stroke. A slow, passionate vibration against my thighs. Echoing in the muggy twilight. I rolled with the groove. Just like Moon Lake. With Paradise. Swinging hip on hip.

Rruumpapa. *Pa-pa*

Rruumpapa. *Pa-pa*

Rruumpapa. *Pa-pa*

Alone on the stage, I kept the groove even. Counting us in. Holding tight to the rhythm.

The guys didn't show.

A soft, steady clap from the crowd lilted onto the stage. Then another. And another. An irresistible call to the passion in the little drum. And when three or four hundred folks joined the beat, downtown Austin shook.

Waylon appeared on the steps to the side of the stage. The band waited. Waylon pressed his hand on Paradise's chest, holding him back until the crowd reached a fevered fist-pumping, hand-clapping, foot-stomping crescendo. This wasn't the count-in we practiced. Waylon left his OCD in Prosper County. He was running the show on pure feel.

Sweat poured down my cheeks. My legs burned from the rope around the *caja*, but I had this corner of downtown Austin on fire and I had yet to roll the sticks on the snare.

Waylon powered onto the stage with Paradise, Cal, and Levi alongside.

Paradise took the mic. "Is it hot enough for you?"

The crowd whistled and whooped.

I kept the beat humming.

Paradise gave Waylon time to plug his Strat into the amp. "Well, it's about to get hotter." He took off his Colombian cowboy hat, waving it in a circle, then growled out, "Waaaay-lon Sliiiiii-der."

And Paradise did something we'd never practiced. He gave up center stage, stepped to the side as Waylon tore into the old Strat. It was like Waylon was plugged into the wall. Playing like a man possessed. He bent the blues out of every string, every fret. And the folks in the crowd rocked and swayed with him as if the melody moved them like reeds in the breeze.

I backed off. Less is more. Levi added a beat with his bass guitar. I set the *caja* down and drew my sticks from my back pocket. This was not at all what we practiced, but going with the flow worked because we owned the flow.

Waylon nodded and Paradise hit his vocals. Waylon was right with him. With the crowd propping up his confidence, Waylon took control of his own lyrics. Singing in his rough, honest way. Paradise faded out as Waylon's voice grew stronger. Paradise made clear whose band it was to anyone watching, but Paradise was nobody's backup singer. He let his accordion be his voice. A deeper layer to the Waylon Slider Band.

I rolled us from one song to another. Driving the beat. Keeping the time.

Cal textured the songs with his light harmony, then hit the Gibson hard. Waylon had the soul; Cal rocked the attitude. He shot a lightning bolt from his guitar that made the hair on my arms stand stiff. Then he danced his fingers along the neck holding a vibrato until my ribs rattled in my chest and the crowd seemed to levitate.

Waylon's voice jammed in and the guys worked into another song.

Paradise accented with his voice and his accordion until a break in the lyrics gave him his time to shine. When the moment was right and Waylon and Cal calmed their guitars. Levi plucked his bass. Paradise punched the bellows on his accordion in short bursts.

I rested my sticks and switched back to the *caja*. The passion.

The crowd found its rhythm again—a pulsing throng—and Paradise took over.

He hugged his accordion to his chest, piling chords on top of chords until his fingers blurred. In one strong-armed, back-bending move, Paradise pulled the bellows in a slow drag across his chest. Letting it exhale. Loud and shrill like a siren. Then he was on. He threw himself into a riff, a jaw-dropping scorcher that crawled up and down, all over my beat.

I caught a glimpse of his grandfather near the corner of the stage. In his eyes, Paradise was a true accordion king. My mother wasn't far from him. She'd stopped fanning herself and was clapping. My mother was clapping.

I suddenly felt like I had the power to tilt the world.

When Paradise, drenched in sweat, panted the bellows to a rest, we all kicked in for the last song. Rocking on Waylon's and Cal's lyrics with the crowd behind us. We played it out. Taking it high at the end—G chords, screaming guitars, tinging cymbals, and the eardrum-frying cry from a smokin' squeezebox.

Lights out.

37

BRANDED

Despite a dark cloud drifting southward, the sun set west of Austin and left in its wake a striking afterglow of dusty pink, lavender, and orange. The most beautiful part of the day isn't always the brightest.

Mother waited for me at the bottom of the steps. The thick makeup under her eyes was gone probably from rubbing away the sweat or her tears. Her eyes were puffy.

She grabbed my shoulders. "Look at you."

I was soaked and my tank top clung to my skin and my bra.

"Your legs." She brushed her hands across the inside of my thigh just above my knee. The rope from the *caja* had shredded my skin, leaving raw, burning stripes.

I hadn't noticed.

"We need paramedics," Mother yelled. "EMS!"

No one paid her any attention. The band showcase was still live, and the band onstage had an electric synthesizer that moaned in loud tones like a foghorn symphony.

"I'm OK." I didn't want to tell her that my thighs felt like they'd been branded. I didn't want to lose the moment. She was there for me. "I'm OK. Really." I winced. "How'd we do?"

She cupped my face in her hands. "I don't know how anyone did but you." Her eyes turned as red as my legs. "You were amazing."

"Excuse me." A tall man in a golf shirt with a shoulder logo that read MEMPHIS SOUND came between us. "I'm a friend of the Sliders'." He gestured toward the radio broadcast booth. Colt Collins was interviewing Waylon as his father stood beside with his arm around Waylon's shoulders.

The man turned to me. "I just met your uncle who tells me you've got a couple years of high school left."

"She does." Mother collected herself.

He handed Mother a business card. "We maintain a stable of studio drummers for recordings across the country, from Nashville to L.A." The man glanced at the band onstage as it limped along to an awkward beat. "Not everyone has the gift of strong timekeeping and adaptability to different styles." He shook my hand then Mother's. "Let us know when you want to come in. We have lots of projects, some small commercial stuff even. We can work with a school schedule till she gets her feet wet and gets some age and experience on her."

Mother stared long and hard at the business card.

My thighs throbbed, but I could've squealed from excitement. "Do I have a job?" I waited while Mother read the card. "Mother?"

"Paisley, honey, I think with the right education you could have a career."

"I knew it. I knew it." I wanted to jump and shout. "All I've ever wanted is to play the drums."

Mother stared across the park at the University tower standing tall against the horizon.

"Not in place of school," I reassured her. "I can do both. Just like Lacey."

As we stood by the stage, folks ran around us and between us. When the area cleared, I saw the guy from Memphis Sound talking to Cal. Nearby, Levi laughed with his brothers as they sipped on longneck bottles. Paradise stood by Estella and wrote his name on some girl's hat. Mother watched them.

"Paisley, the music business isn't going to be a Sunday stroll down a blacktop road. They don't call it a boulevard of broken dreams for nothing." She tucked the card in her purse. "A lot of people, a lot of talented kids, get really messed up and go off on wild, loose tangents and never find their way back."

I sensed her protective walls closing around me. "Kids not in the music business get messed up too." My chest tightened as I remembered Lacey passed out in the backseat of the Bronco. "Depends on the kid."

Mother pushed her thick hair away from her face. A bead of sweat inched down her cheek, etching a crooked scar in her makeup. "If you're waiting for me to say your dad and I messed up, don't hold your breath."

"You don't have to say it." I called her hand. "You judge everybody and calculate every step Lacey and I make on your own mistakes."

Mother raised her voice. "And you don't think our experience is worth learning from?"

"Your experience has taught me to chase my dreams and not let anything get in the way of that."

The last band closed out. Colt Collins and Jaybird took the stage to announce the showcase winners.

"The music business was good enough for you when you pushed Lacey to sing." I stood my ground. "Don't tell me you're not going to support me."

"I'll be there every step of the way," she promised. Or warned, I wasn't sure. "We're just going to take teeny, tiny baby steps. This doesn't have to be a footrace."

High and above the crowd, a band of girls squealed so loud the crackles settling in for the night burst from the park trees. The all-girl band won the Texapalooza Youth Showcase.

"I've got to find Waylon."

Mother followed me as I gingerly moved through the crowd, careful not to rub my thighs against each other. The burning had almost turned numb.

The boys hung together along with a crowd of folks. Paradise had his arm around his grandfather, but dropped it and came running toward me. He picked me up and spun me around. I tried not to scream when my thighs brushed against his jeans.

"Put her down," Mother ordered. "Down!"

I patted him on his back. "My legs."

He let me down and saw the swollen bands where the *caja* had cut into my thighs.

Paradise knelt down and rubbed his finger around the swollen part just above my knee.

"That's enough." Mother shooed him back.

Waylon and the other guys walked up.

"We let her play too long." Paradise had his hands on hips. "She stayed in the pocket with the ropes slicing her legs just so we could make a bigger entrance."

"Sorry, Paisley." Waylon's skull cap was off and his hair was as wild as his guitar playing. "I had no idea."

"I'm OK. It's my fault for wearing shorts." My legs continued to ache. I really didn't want everyone staring at my thighs. "I'm sorry we lost."

Waylon's father rushed up with a bag of ice. I took it and held it against one leg.

"I don't know who you think lost," Waylon's father drawled. "Those girls have been playing the Austin circuit for years. They've got a table set up with CDs on the other side of the stage."

Levi laughed. "We lost to some home cooking."

I switched the cold bag to my other leg.

"Y'all made a name for yourselves." He squeezed Waylon's neck and the pride just burst through Waylon's smile. "You made a name with good, solid playing. That wins every time."

The pastel colors in the sky intensified as the sun set lower.

The soft voice belonging to Paradise's grandfather drifted in. "Gabriela, you have to go."

I pulled the ice pack off. "Go where?"

All of us, the whole group stared at him.

Paradise looked down at his boots, then grinned like a barn cat. His cheek dimpled deep enough for a coin slot. "Los Tres Reyes. The Tejano trio?" He smiled as if we all knew who he was talking about.

"Grammy winners." Uncle L. V. helped him out.

Paradise took off his hat and rolled the brim. "They caught me as I came offstage." He put the hat back on. "I'm going to play accordion for them at a Cinco de Mayo celebration in Houston. I'm flying out with them tonight."

The boys congratulated him in their fist-bumping, bromance kind of way.

I hugged him, but I had to laugh. "You know you have to get on a plane to fly?"

"Yes." He reached for my hand and clasped my fingers in his, tucking our hands behind his back where Mother couldn't see. "But it's not going to be some war relic we have to land in a pasture."

Uncle L. V. pointed at us. "Your boy there can catch a ride to the airport with us. We're going to need to get *Miss Molly* up and headed east."

Paradise leaned down and breathed onto my neck. "Did he just call me your boy?"

He held my hand as we followed L. V. and Mother out of the park. High on adrenaline and the success of drumming at Texapalooza, I walked beside him forgetting about the pain in my legs.

"I guess if I'm your boy"—Paradise kissed the top of my head— "what does that make you?"

—CAL'S LYRIC JOURNAL—

SIX STRINGS AND A HEART FOR YOU

The crowd heard you first, but for me they screamed
I'm high on that rush, it's what I've dreamed
But what goes up comes down and when I turned around
I had a hold on my guitar, you couldn't be found

This is how I do
Six strings and a heart for you
Picking out a melody, playing it through
Some place away from the crowd and the noise
I should tell you I care, but I can't find the voice
This is how I do
Six strings and a heart for you

We're heading back home, but it won't be the same
Me and my boys, only a mention of your name
It would've been sweet to have you along
But when he took your hand, I knew you were gone

Some place away from the crowd and the noise
I should tell you I ~~love~~ care, but I can't find the voice
So this is how I do
Six strings and a heart for you

38

SWEET GOOD-BYE

While Mother chatted on the phone to Dad and Uncle L. V. turned in a flight plan, I snuck outside with Paradise.

The thunderstorms that skirted around Austin during Texapalooza had drifted southeast, leaving us with a cool breeze and a clear night. We found a bench where we could watch the planes take off and land.

Paradise pulled my legs across his lap. He rubbed his fingers softly over the red welts. "I can't believe you stayed in the pocket."

"Yes, you can." I flicked at the gold ring dangling from his ear. "I didn't even know the rope was cutting. Once the crowd started, I jumped to a whole new level of consciousness."

Paradise slid his arm along the back of the bench and leaned into me. "I was good, wasn't I?"

I laughed as a plane touched down. "Greatness. Sheer greatness."

"No." He waved off my observation. "That was Waylon." Paradise shook his head. "What got into him?"

"I think he's always had it. He'd just never broken free and let it all out. You helped him along."

Paradise watched a plane race down the runway and lift off. "Wide-open. That's how it's got to be."

"And you're OK with flying to Houston?"

He fiddled with my ring, turning it on my finger. "That's how it's got to be."

"Paisley," Uncle L. V. hollered from the doorway. "*Miss Molly's* ready, so's that DC-3 your boy's flyin' in."

We stood up. Paradise faced me and rested his fingers on the fullest part of my backside. "You didn't answer me earlier. If I'm your boy, what does that make you?"

"Boss."

He cocked that little barn cat grin again. "OK, Boss." He cleared his throat. "When I get back, I'm going to take you to Moon Lake and let you tell me *no* some more."

I kissed him. "When you get back and take me to Moon Lake, I will tell you *no* some more." I had all I could handle figuring out my place in the world. No matter what, *yes* would be a long time coming.

Paradise tugged on my hand. I felt my ring leave my finger.

He took his necklace off and slid my ring onto the chain. "'One Life, One Love.' When girls start throwing themselves at me, I may need this as a reminder of what's waiting back home."

We took our time going inside. "I'm telling my mother you stole my ring. She already thinks you stole one of L. V.'s hats."

"You better tell your mother to nail down everything she cares about. She don't know what I might run off with." He hugged me one last time. "Moon Lake. Think about it."

I pressed my ear to his heart. I'd remember that beat forever.

39

SMOKE AND ASH

I could always find a rhythm. A cycling air conditioner in a quiet house. A frog's ribbet at the edge of a still pond. The steady thumping of my own heart.

But when I heard Uncle L. V.'s voice in my house on Monday morning when he should've been on a run to Houston and the only time he didn't make a run to Houston was in bad weather and he was in my house and it wasn't even Christmas we were nowhere near Christmas or December and when I saw my mother with her hand over her mouth and my dad with both hands pressed onto the table like if he pushed hard enough everything would stop and L. V. wouldn't stop talking about plane crashes and musicians and DC-3s and Ricky Nelson and that there was nothing left but smoke and ash . . .

I couldn't find a beat anywhere.

Not even in my own chest.

I broke in two. Like one of those candy straws that you snap and all the candy comes pouring out leaving nothing but an empty straw. Nothing left.

No amount of sorrys would ever make things right, would ever bring Paradise back.

And the phone could keep ringing and Lacey could keep telling Levi and Waylon and Cal and anybody else who asked that I was strung out. She hadn't seen strung out yet. I didn't care about anything anymore. The band. The drums. When a life is gone, it's gone.

Paradise was gone.

40

A HEARTBEAT AWAY

"Get her up, Diane." Uncle L. V.'s voice came from our kitchen for the second time in a matter of days. "You can't let her lay in there forever."

Mother whispered some excuse for me.

I was sick of hearing them talk about me. I walked into the kitchen, following the smell of warm vanilla. She had a pound cake in the oven. My favorite.

"Put some jeans on, Paisley." Uncle L. V. rubbed his mustache. "I disked the ruts in my pasture and drug it back to level this morning. You get to sow the seed and fertilizer."

"I'll help you another day."

"Another day and weeds'll take root." He pointed to the door. "You caused the mess. You'll make it right. Today."

"Let the weeds take over. I don't care about your pasture."

Mother doused a bowl of strawberries in sugar. She might make my favorite dessert, but she'd leave me to fight my own battle with L. V.

"My pasture doesn't care about your feelings either." L. V. turned the doorknob. "I'll be waiting." He shut the door behind him.

I stomped to my room, threw on a pair of jeans. *I'd sow his freakin' seed and be done with it. With him.*

Mother clanked around in the kitchen. From the noise it sounded like she lost her favorite frying pan. A lid crashed to the floor and spun. I knew it was a lid because nothing else came that close to a cymbal.

"Take a snack. You haven't eaten lunch." She handed me a brown paper sack on my way out the door. "Paisley." She brushed a wave of hair from her face. "Don't give up on yourself."

I cut through the woods on the four-wheeler. Pine straw covered the trail and the hard ride over it stirred up the evergreen scent. I burst out of the woods and saw the hangar on top of the hill. I turned my head. Didn't even want to look. The band and Texapalooza and Paradise. I couldn't think about any of it without feeling like I wanted to curl up, sleep it off. And pray that when I woke up, Paradise would be a heartbeat away.

I parked the four-wheeler by L. V.'s house and walked down to the pasture. Uncle L. V. waited, like he said. He had a rectangle half the size of a football field turned over in a rich black dirt. The tractor was nowhere in sight. Just L. V in a sombrero standing by a cooler.

"Strap into that." He pointed to a hand seeder with shoulder braces and a bucket on the front deep enough to hold a twenty-pound bag of seed.

"You want me to hand seed this whole area?"

"No." L. V. took a frozen candy bar from the cooler. "I want my field of clover back. But since I can't have that, I expect to enjoy a green patch of Bermuda grass in June. Hand seeding keeps you from tearing up the rest of the pasture with the tractor."

I hooked the straps over my shoulders. L. V. handed me a pair of gloves. I shoved my hands in them and made a fist.

He tucked the candy bar in his shirt pocket and glared at me. "Seed don't spread any faster mad than it does when you're glad." He poured half a sack of Bermuda seed into the spreader.

The weight pulled me forward. I pictured Paradise in my mind. How strong he was and how easy he made playing the accordion look. Like it was tin-can light.

"I need some water." I choked back tears.

Uncle L. V. didn't believe in bottled water. He handed me a jug with ice cubes swishing around the inside. I turned it up and gulped down a swig.

I set out, turning the crank and spinning seed across the tilled field. Uncle L. V. trailed behind me—half of a seed sack in one hand, the water jug in the other. Walking over the turned-up soil took balance and it took a rhythm. A step-sink, step-sink. A little like walking on a boat. I stepped in time, up and down, back around until L. V. stopped me. I'd sown half the section.

The sun beat down on us. He pitched me the jug.

"I am sorry about your pasture."

Uncle L. V. took off his sombrero and fanned us up a breeze. "Clover's not coming back, Paisley."

I started to cry. I didn't want to. I just couldn't stop. I didn't know when the crying would ever stop.

"But this pasture is still here. It's strong. It's healthy. I can have Bermuda in June. Oats for the deer in fall." He dumped the rest of the seed in the spreader.

I turned the crank and started walking. Step, sink. Step, sink. Paradise was gone. I tried to remember the smell of his shirt, the way his hair curled with just a mist of sweat, the pillowy softness of his lips. Remembering was like trying to catch leaves in the fall. The moment I reached for it, to hold, the instant it drifted.

I scattered the seed over the ground. We'd made round after round on into the afternoon when Waylon's Camaro bounced over the cattle guard. Levi in his truck and Cal riding shotgun followed behind Waylon. The pipes from Levi's truck rumbled as he switched gears on his way up the hill to the hangar.

L. V. didn't look surprised. He knew they were coming. He probably called them.

"I can't go," I told L. V. "It doesn't seem right. It hurts too much."

L. V. lifted the spreader off my shoulders and laid it on the ground. "You've still got dreams and a future. You're the same drummer you've always been." He shaded us with his sombrero. "That all-girl band from Austin even called your momma. They want a new drummer."

I took the gloves off and wiped my cheek. "I bet it took her all of three seconds to hang up on them."

"Actually, Jack said she stayed on the line for a good minute. Then she said *no*."

Any other time and I'd have milked goats to get to drum for a band like that. I would've been furious with Mother.

When the boys rolled the hangar doors open, the grating *dit-dit-dit-dit-dit* echoed across the pasture.

I had no desire to be part of another band.

L. V. kicked some dirt over the seed. "I'll drag this over and finish for you. When you get to the hangar, you'll find something on your snare." He scratched his belly. "Your boy's grandfather brought it by. Said he wanted you to have it."

41

FINDING THE GROOVE

From outside the hangar, I could hear Waylon trying new chords on his Strat. He knew how to bend a string until a tear fell out.

My boots clapped across the concrete as I moved toward the drums.

Waylon stopped playing.

Levi twirled his hat on the end of one of my drumsticks. "How are your legs?"

"Better," I said, walking slowly toward my drum kit.

Resting across the snare was a stick a few inches longer than my drumstick. It looked like a trimmed pole of pure Louisiana sugar cane. The *guacharaca*. Beside it was a forklike thing with metal tines and a wooden handle. If I hadn't known better, I would've thought it was one of Lacey's hair picks.

But I knew better.

And I knew the reason it belonged to me was because I could play it with a broken heart. *Congratulations to me.* The *guacharaca* felt more like a cruel punishment than a present.

I picked it up anyway. It was the first instrument I had held in my hands in days.

The boys watched me and I wondered if they knew what it was, what it meant.

I traced the wood with my finger first. It was smooth except for the notched ridges scarred into the sides. I dragged the wire fork down the stick and back. *Scritch-scratch. Scritch-scratch.*

"Paisley." Waylon stood beside me with one of his band notebooks. "We've been working on some new material," he explained. "We called you, but Lacey kept telling us . . ."

I held my palm up and closed my eyes. I did not want to hear his rundown of why I hadn't taken their calls. I lived it.

Levi stretched his arm out. "I'm gonna play with y'all until you find another bass player or I head off to summer workouts."

That wasn't new information. "What you really mean is that you're giving us a sympathy pass and not walking out right now because Paradise is gone and that would be two holes to fill." I scraped the stick some more.

"We all hurt, Paisley." Levi put his hat on his head and handed me my drumstick. "You don't have the lockdown on that."

I put the drumstick down and rolled the *guacharaca* over the tops of my legs. I ran my finger along the ridges. "I don't have it in me to play right now."

"Play when you heal." Waylon sat on a stool and thumbed a string. "Or play to heal." He picked a chorus of chords out of the Strat.

Cal's Gibson was still in its case. Cal sat in a chair with his head tossed back and stared at the rafters. He thumped his spiral with his pencil. I'd heard his songs after he and Waylon added the melodies. I'd even seen them writing together.

Levi and Waylon tinkered on their guitars. With the *guacharaca* in my hand, I knelt beside Cal. His spiral open to a page with just the words *Until Then*.

I borrowed his pencil and his spiral. He leaned down to help me.

—CAL'S LYRIC JOURNAL—
(with Paisley)

Now you're gone
I'm done
I'm long gone, ripped apart, a wildflower
in the wind.

Someday there's hope
I know
It'll find me one day soon and I'll stand
strong once again.
I'll be able to stand the wind.

Until then

42

DON'T STOP

Lacey layered herself in perfume that smelled remarkably like Mother's pound cake. She showered with the gel, buttered herself up with a creamy lotion in the same scent, powdered any of her parts that might sweat, then finished it all off with a spritzing of eau de vanilla.

She'd never had an official date before.

From the smell of things, Lacey apparently thought the way to Levi's heart was through his stomach.

"You smell good enough to eat." I sat on her bed feeling hungry. "I hope you don't draw flies."

"That would be plain awful." Lacey tied her halter dress at the neck and turned around. "Am I even?" She looked down at her cleavage.

"No wonky boobs." I watched her smooth her dress and step into her heels.

"Remember those matching halter dresses we wore at Easter?" Lacey giggled. "They were those Easter egg colors and Gabri . . ." Her voice trailed off. "Sorry."

I shook my head and picked at the embroidery on her pillow. "It happens." And it did. Weeks had gone by but the mention of his name was like pulling a scab off a wound and the bleeding starting all over again.

"I could stay home with you tonight." Lacey sat beside me.

I laughed out loud. Couldn't keep from it. "OK, you do that."

"All right, I'm not about to stay here." Lacey grabbed her phone and put it in a small beaded handbag that she'd lifted from Mother's closet. "But you can call me and I'll talk to you."

"That's comforting." I held on to the pillow, my fingers tapped out a one-two-three, one-two-three beat against the soft back.

The doorbell rang.

"Levi," Lacey squeaked. "You gotta beat Mother to the door!" She shoved me out of her room.

Lacey didn't have to worry about me beating Mother to the door. Mother sat in the living room BeDazzling the pocket on a pair of her jeans. Dad answered the door.

"Paisley." Levi nodded and spoke to me as if we had no history. I could've tap-danced on his starched shirt, and he had on nice boots. But I'd bet a hundred bucks his baseball cap was on his truck dash and would be on his head before he and Lacey made it down the drive.

Levi presented Mother with a bottle of wine. The label on it read, TUCKER VINEYARDS. "That's our best stock."

Mother held the bottle by the neck. "I'm sure it is."

Levi tried to make conversation. "My mom thought you'd like the red more than the white. She said she remembered when y'all were younger that you liked drinks with color more."

Dad faked a cough.

I remembered the Purple Jesus punch that Paradise warned me about at the Tucker Barn. And I remembered how he touched my face in the rain.

"That's very considerate." Mother smiled with her lips together like the Grinch's. "I'm glad to know her memory survived her youth."

The sweet smell of vanilla drifted into the living room and Lacey followed behind it. Not a hair out of place. She was perfect. Like a porcelain doll.

Levi took her hand, kissed her cheek. "You"—he caught his breath—"you look beautiful."

Lacey rose up on her tiptoes as if she'd burst into flight. Mother held the wine bottle like Dad would hold a hammer. He pulled Mother to him, nuzzled her neck, and took the bottle away from her.

And all I wanted to do was go to Moon Lake and dance one more time.

When they left, Mother uncorked the Tucker wine. "God, if this kills me, don't let L. V. convince y'all to bury me in the peach orchard. And I don't want the Slider Brothers playing at my funeral." Mother winced like she'd stepped on a rusty nail. "I'm sorry, Paisley."

"Please don't apologize every time you talk about death." I wondered when the sorrys would stop. If they ever would. I wanted to be able to remember Paradise without the memory always being punctuated by a sad-faced oopsie.

Mother mumbled to herself about Levi and Lacey and dating.

"If you hate Lacey going out with Levi so much, why'd you let her go?"

She looked at Dad. "Because regret is a hard thing to live with. That's why." She poured the wine in a glass and sniffed it. "I regret a lot of my choices, but not the big ones. I absolutely do not regret loving your dad or you girls." Mother sipped the wine as if it were vinegar and pushed it away.

"She regrets not following through with her dream," Dad spoke up. "She wanted to be a chef. And she could've done it too, but she put it all on the back burner for us."

"Jack, stop." Mother fidgeted.

"And your Texapalooza stunt got me to thinking." He pulled a folded piece of paper from his wallet. "Lacey and I figured up the cost of her beauty school plus her community college tuition. Those folks at the Bible college appreciated the fancy food we catered." Dad handed the paper to Mother. "They said they'd pay for you to cater their monthly concert." He pointed. "The figure at the top is Lacey's school. The figure in the middle is what Lacey told them you'd charge."

"My gosh." Mother's eyes widened. "That's high."

I peeked. "Wow. That's a Lacey number all right."

"You're worth that and more," Dad said.

Mother moved her rhinestones and BeDazzler to the floor. "What's this number at the bottom?"

"That's the estimate on a kitchen renovation that I'm paying for, and you'll need in order to get your catering company off the ground."

Mother shook her head. "I can't. The girls."

"They're growing up. You've always wanted to do this and the money can help pay for their school. I know you can be great." Dad wound his arm around himself, rubbed his shoulder. "No excuses about Prosper County being too small or Dripping Springs being in the middle of nowhere. This is your time."

Mother clutched the paper to her chest. Her face lit up with possibilities that she'd pushed down for years and years.

I had my drumsticks in my back pocket. Even though I hadn't played in weeks, I kept them close because I was too afraid to put them down. Scared I'd never pick them back up.

I pulled them out. Gripped them.

Outside, the days were longer, and it was still plenty light in the west.

I called Waylon and Cal to meet me at the hangar. Cal answered the phone like I hadn't talked to him in a year. "Hey, girl. It's been a long time," he said.

I set out. For the hangar. For the drums. For whatever the future held. Texapalooza wasn't the dream come true; it was the dream taking off.

A rhythm I couldn't escape hung in the air. I heard a heartbeat I'd never forget. It would always be with me. I set my stride to the pulse in my memory and pushed on. Wide-open.

The sweet smell of the first hay of the season drifted across the pasture. I walked to the hangar. I wanted the feel of the Prosper County dirt beneath my boots. I wanted to breathe under the broad night sky. I wanted to drum. I wanted to dance—if not at the pier, somewhere. The sun had gone, disappeared, pulling a trail of darkness over us all. But a crescent moon, a silver sliver, floated above the horizon. And Venus burned next to it. She shines the brightest right after the sunset.

—CAL'S LYRIC JOURNAL—
with Paisley and Waylon

GOOD MOURNING SONG

You left before I could say good-bye
Time rolls on and so do I
You taught us to trust in our best, own the moment,
   screw the rest
You'd expect nothing less
Than for us to write you a good mourning song.

The sun comes up and I want to cry
Shake a fist at God, and wonder why
But you'd find that a waste of time, put on your boots,
   and move along
You would move along
Taking with you your good mourning song.

You showed me things aren't always what they seem
One man's hobby is another man's dream
You were wild rides and warm sweet kisses
You were burn the candle at both ends and make two wishes
You'd leave no regrets
So this is your good mourning song.

We're still taking the drums and guitars high
Rolling with your spirit that stayed behind
So the door slammed, we'll bust a window
Go wide-open, a bright beyond
And we will sing your good mourning song.
A new day, and this good morning song.

ACKNOWLEDGMENTS

From the muse that is country music to a bound book with a rockin' cover, I get by with a little help from my friends:

My agent, Michael Bourret, who encouraged me to put my stamp on the "band book" genre. Boot-stamped.

My editor, Liz Szabla, whose patience and guidance delivered the melody of *Paradise* to me.

The teams/roadies at the Society of Children's Books Writers and Illustrators, and Feiwel and Friends, whose support is as steady as the backbeat to a song.

My jam session/critique partners, Erin, Linda, Martha, and Sharon, who know how to get down to the nitty-gritty.

Friends and groupies, including Stacy and Blake, Katie and Sarah, Craig and Catherine, who not only read, but cheer me up.

My husband, Jon, who believes when I can't, and holds my hand as we run this dream down.

And the forever fun-loving William, my son, who has both endured and survived socially despite my carpool tendencies to blare Southern rock and country with the windows wide open. *Hey, hey, Big Red. . . . It's how I roll!*

Thanks, y'all.